TWO YEARS AFTER

PAUL J. TEAGUE

ALSO BY PAUL J. TEAGUE

Morecambe Bay Trilogy 1

Book 1 - Left For Dead

Book 2 - Circle of Lies

Book 3 - Truth Be Told

Morecambe Bay Trilogy 2

Book 4 - Trust Me Once

Book 5 - Fall From Grace

Book 6 - Bound By Blood

Morecambe Bay Trilogy 3

Book 7 - First To Die

Book 8 - Nothing To Lose

Book 9 - Last To Tell

Note: The Morecambe Bay trilogies are best read in the order shown above.

Don't Tell Meg Trilogy

Features DCI Kate Summers and Steven Terry.

Book 1 - Don't Tell Meg

Book 2 - The Murder Place

Book 3 - The Forgotten Children

Standalone Thrillers

Dead of Night

One Last Chance

No More Secrets

So Many Lies

Friends Who Lie

Now You See Her

PROLOGUE

London – February 2017, 23:17

Rosie watched the first drop of blood splash onto the shattered windscreen below her. It appeared to be making the journey in slow motion, but she knew that was just an illusion, caused by the impact of the crash. In her barely conscious state, it seemed surreal. Half an hour earlier they'd been enjoying canapés and laughing at David Willis' new goatee beard. At his age, he ought to know better.

Liam was still, completely still. She couldn't even hear his breathing. Her arms were numb; she tried to reach over to him, to touch him, to check if he was still alive, but she couldn't find the strength. The engine was running, the lights dipped but still shining out ahead of them. She could see grass, a fence and a tree. That's what must have caused the startling jolt which jarred her neck.

Why was nobody coming to help them? Why was it taking so long for help to arrive? Didn't they know about the babies? Were they still safe inside her?

She could feel the pressure of the seat belt pushing hard into the bump in her stomach. Please let the babies be okay.

As Rosie struggled to stay awake for Liam's sake, she tried to recall the lovely evening they'd just had, running through the events in sequence, forcing her mind to focus. She had to be awake when help arrived. She needed to tell them that Liam was AB negative, the rarest blood type. It would be a problem. Those vital seconds would count. She had to stay awake, not only for Liam's sake but also for the babies.

It had been such a happy gathering, the perfect ending before her maternity leave and a wonderful send-off for Gina. And David's promise to her was the icing on the cake.

Rosie forced herself to recount what had happened, in the precise order that it occurred. If she could do that, it meant she was still alive, and that her body was working well enough for her to get through this. She could hear a siren far off in the distance; was it for them?

She'd already had her own leaving party, but with Gina Saloman finally off on her travels, Rosie couldn't resist showing her face, even though she was thirty-four weeks pregnant and feeling very heavy with it. It was the source of many jokes from the guys in the sales team, but she didn't care.

Having twins was the best news they could have had, after trying so long. They deserved this. She'd even managed to drag Liam along to the party with her, which in itself warranted a herald of bugles. He was always a quiet one, Liam. But she loved him, and when they were together, he emerged from his shell, bright, funny and confident.

The siren was coming closer. The blood was dripping faster. Drip – drip – drip, an annoying interruption to her thoughts. It was coming from Liam, but she couldn't see his injury.

'Liam... Liam. Can you hear me? Try to move if you can. They're coming. The ambulance is coming. They'll get us out of here. The babies will be fine.'

Rosie felt herself drifting again. She forced herself back into awareness; she needed to stay awake. If she let herself fade, she couldn't help Liam, and she was no use to him if she passed out. The pain was so bad that all she wanted to do was melt away from it. A few more minutes, stay with Liam just a few more minutes. Make sure the babies aren't hurt.

She'd been jealous of Gina Saloman at first, leaving work like that, with only a rucksack, her laptop and a dream. Heading for Spain, setting up her own nomadic business, hoping to leave the workplace for good. Gina's future life would be everything that Rosie's wouldn't be. She was about to lose her freedom, but it was what she and Liam had chosen. When they'd discovered it was twins, they couldn't have been more ecstatic. An entire family at one sitting. The doctors had said that might happen with fertility drugs.

Gina had been a popular member of the team at Willis Supplies Ltd, so it had been a good turnout for her leaving do. They were all there, helping themselves to the free booze amid a tirade of sexist and tasteless jokes from the sales guys, as if equal rights and workplace rules had never happened. David had laid on quite a spread. He liked Gina; everybody knew that. She'd be a big loss to the business.

She could see the flashing of blue lights and a glimpse of a red fire engine. Thank God. They'd get the two of them – no, the *four* of them – out of that crumpled wreck and into a hospital. And what about that man who was walking on the pavement? Where was he? Was he the person who alerted the emergency services?

They would stop Liam's bleeding. The blood bank would have his blood type and he'd be saved. Then the doctors would check the babies and give them the all-clear. They'd get through this. If she could only stay awake, they'd make it out, she was certain.

Gina. Think of Gina's party. Stay awake.

There had been so much happiness at the leaving event, and she couldn't recall when she'd last seen everybody having such a good time. It had been a masterstroke loading up with party poppers, cardboard hats, blowers and even a piñata. She'd thought she was going into labour when she saw how Terry Fincham had sabotaged the piñata; he'd replaced the candy with a selection of sex aids.

There had been gasps of astonishment as a small vibrator, a packet of exotic condoms, a vibrating ring and a hostile-looking butt plug had tumbled to the ground, accompanied by a tube of Smarties and a Mars Bar. Terry knew how to get a party going. After the gasps of shock had turned into laughter, the Prosecco came out, and they were away: raucous laughter, filthy jokes and office banter.

Was Liam drunk? She couldn't remember. Would they find he was over the limit? Surely they'd save him first and breathalyse him later. They wouldn't waste time, considering his injuries. Or could they tell from his blood? She didn't know. She'd never been in a car accident before.

At the sound of voices, Rosie wanted to cry with relief. At last she could pass over the responsibility for Liam to someone else. She didn't have to be the strong one for all of them – the firefighters would take the strain.

There was a female voice; she hadn't expected that.

'Does it hurt? Are you okay? What about your partner? Is he your husband?'

Rosie felt herself drifting again. Why was her rescuer upside down? No, she and Liam were upside down – the car had flipped. The firefighter was speaking to her through the shattered window to her side.

'We're going to have to cut you out, my love. You're safe now, we've got you. Try to hang on a little longer. We'll get you out, don't worry.'

A few minutes more, that's all she needed to manage. Then she could sleep. They'd pack her off in an ambulance, give her something for the pain, and congratulate her on the babies. She'd wake up hours later, and it would all be fine. And Liam would be conscious. They'd stitch up his cuts. The blood was beginning to pool now; they'd need to attend to that straight away.

David Willis had offered her a promotion at the party. It couldn't have come at a better time.

'Of course, it stands for when you're back from maternity leave,' he'd told her with a smile. 'Come back to the office whenever you're ready, and when you do, you can have that corner office. It's yours, Rosie. Just make sure you don't get too caught up with the twins and decide never to come back to work again.'

'We can't afford to do that.' She'd laughed. 'A small terraced house in London costs a fortune. Liam and I will be working until we're a hundred years old before we get it paid off.'

The extra money would certainly make life easier when she returned to the office.

'We're cutting your husband out first.'

It was a male voice, deep and confident.

'Stay with us, my darling. You'll hear a horrible noise in

a moment, but it's just the cutters. They won't hurt you. I'll be with you all the time.'

The woman was still there. Rosie could see her face, peering through the hole where the glass had been.

As the noise of the cutters filled her ears, Rosie became aware of more people moving around outside, talking urgently. A blinding light shone from lamps trained on the vehicle. She couldn't move her head to get a good look at Liam. The air was filled with the violent sounds of creaking and grinding metal as part of the roof was wrenched back and they cut through the pillars to his front and side.

'He's AB negative,' Rosie said, but she couldn't make herself heard.

'She's pregnant.'

'Jesus Christ.'

There were worried mutterings outside.

'Let the ambulance team know and make sure the hospital is clear about what's coming in.'

'Heavily pregnant too,' came the woman's voice. 'About to pop, if you ask me.'

Rosie had forgotten to mention the babies. She assumed everybody knew, just by looking at her. She'd been so worried about Liam that she'd forgotten about herself.

Outside the car, the voices were sounding more concerned.

'We need to move over to the woman's side. She's the priority.'

'We're going to be cutting close to your head, my darling,' said the woman. 'Try to blank out the sound. Close your eyes too; it will protect you from any broken glass.'

A hand came through the shattered screen and squeezed her arm. It was warm and reassuring, the female firefighter reaching out as best as she could before the cutting began. She was making sure the children were okay.

'It won't be long – we'll have you and the baby out in no time,' she said.

'Babies.' Rosie replied. 'It's babies.'

The cutting began, and she closed her eyes, remembering Gina's beaming face as they sent her off on her adventures.

That'll be us soon, she'd thought to herself. *Me and Liam. We'll have smiling faces like that, and people will be happy for us too.*

Rosie was aware of Liam being manoeuvred out of his seat to her side. She couldn't turn to look because her neck was in so much pain. She also heard more concerned voices. Something about a pedestrian.

Why wasn't Liam helping them? Why did they have to pull him like that? She willed him on silently. *Help them, Liam, help them get you out.*

'Just a couple more minutes,' the female voice said in a soothing voice. 'We've got an ambulance team on standby; you and your baby will be in safe hands in no time.'

'Babies,' Rosie insisted again, frustrated that she couldn't make herself heard. 'Babies.'

As the heavy cutters tore through the metal structure to her side, she suddenly realised. The babies. They'd been lively all evening, as if they couldn't wait to get out into the world and start their lives. But ever since the crash, she hadn't felt them moving. They were completely still.

Trinity Heights Psychiatric Hospital – May 2018, 21:48

. . .

Rosie sensed Vera Philpot was checking up on her, but as she drifted in and out of consciousness, it was hard to follow what was happening and where Vera was in the room.

This drug regime was exactly what she wanted; it shut down her mind, blanked her thoughts and rendered her body useless. She could lie there, all day and night, barely aware of the passage of time. With Sam a ward of court and in the care of her father, and the inquests and funerals out of the way, she could abdicate all responsibility. The culmination of it all was sweet relief when it came: a bungled attempt at suicide at the flyover, being sectioned in Trinity Heights and a cocktail of drugs which dulled the pain.

Every shred of dignity was gone. The woman she was, the responsibility she'd managed, the salary she'd commanded – none of it mattered. Her world was broken. All there was to look forward to was the paradise of oblivion and the feeling that she didn't have to do anything. Everything was taken care of.

The money, the baby and the job could all wait. First, she had to get her head straight.

Vera was the perfect nurse to have on the ward. She was gentle, reassuring and kind. She reminded Rosie of her mum. How she still missed her. She'd have known what to do. Vera had made her feel more confident that she wouldn't try to jump again. She'd convinced her she had to hang on for Sam's sake; he needed to know his mother. But Vera also made the agony slip away. It was she who brought the pills, arriving like an angel to make Rosie forget.

'I'm just going to throw out these flowers that your dad brought. They've all wilted. I'll be back soon.'

Rosie couldn't even remember her father visiting. Had he come with Sam?

'Back again! Here are your clothes from the laundry. I'll

hang them on your chair. Maybe you can try to put them in the wardrobe later?'

It felt like Vera was only gone for a matter of seconds, but as she focused on the digital clock on her bedside table, Rosie saw that she'd been on her own for an hour or more. And if Vera thought she was up to getting out of bed, she was badly mistaken. It was as much as she could do to open her eyes.

Vera was gone again. But there was a movement in the room. Rosie tried to prise her eyes open. She'd had a lovely dream, that she was a little girl and she and her mother were cooking. She wanted to be back there, at a happy time, away from the realities of the present.

Someone was touching her leg. Was she being bed-bathed? The drugs had kicked in. She couldn't fight the tiredness. But somebody was running their hand up her bare legs. They were smooth hands, a woman's perhaps. And she couldn't move her mouth to ask them to stop.

She woke again, not sure how long afterwards. She couldn't even see who it was. They were stroking her hair. Who was stroking her hair? Nobody would do that except Liam, and he was dead. She shut out the thought and forced the darkness away from her mind, drifting off again.

Where was Vera? She wanted Vera back. Who was this person in the room? If only she could wake up properly.

Rosie heard Vera's voice along the corridor, attending to the patient in the next room. She didn't even know her neighbour's name yet, and she didn't care. Just getting through the day was enough to cope with.

The person who was with her in the room tensed when Vera's voice became audible, as she made her way back. Were they even supposed to be there? Through the haze of oblivion, Rosie's heart quickened. What if this person meant her harm? She couldn't move, couldn't even cry out. As she faded back into nothingness, she sensed the person moving towards the door. They were speaking, but the words were distorted in her head, echoing around her mind so that wasn't even sure whether she'd imagined it.

'I'll be back, Rosie. We're not done yet. I like it when you're all mine. I like it when we're alone, and I can do what I want to you.'

CHAPTER ONE

She'd had better days. Her only consolation was that she'd also experienced much worse – terrible, dark, frightening days. And lots of them.

Sam appeared to have saved up every bit of toddler bad behaviour possible just for that morning. Her first day back at work in two years. Two years! It seemed incredible.

Rosie looked at the checklist she'd prepared the day before to help her dad manage everything. Potty – snacks – wipes – toys – emergency contact numbers. She was sure it was all there. They were blundering through this together, but at least she only had to survive for two days that week. Thank goodness her first day back was on a Thursday.

She took a glass from the worktop and half-filled it with water, then fumbled around inside her bag until she found the box she was looking for. Duloxetine, the only thing that would get her through the door of that high-rise office and past the first day.

She gulped down her pill and added a couple of Ibuprofen to the mix. There was no way she'd get through the day without the usual cocktail of drugs that she'd relied on since the accident to dull the pain. She barely knew what she was mixing any more, but there'd be plenty of time to wean herself off them.

Sam threw his half-gnarled banana on the floor and began to scream at her, as if he could sense what she was feeling inside. If she could have taken all her fear, anxiety, depression and sadness and rolled it into one human being, it would have looked like Sam at that very moment.

There was a knock at the door. Her poor dad, sacrificing his retirement for a seven o'clock start. She handed Sam his non-spill beaker and rushed to the door.

'Hi Dad!' she said, moving in to give him a hug. He'd always been such a strong man, but he felt so thin these days.

'How are you, Rosie? Up for the challenge of the day?'

She shrugged. He knew she wasn't ready for it; they both did. But what choice did they have? Everything had run out, including her maternity pay. If only she'd got some compensation from the accident. But no, she was on her own and she had to work. She'd thought of moving her dad in with her, but one of them would have to sleep on the couch. He was in council housing too, he couldn't afford to lose that at his age, however tough things were getting.

'I'm sorry to drag you out so early, Dad. But I want to go and see Liam before I go into work. It'll make me feel better, what with it being such a big day.'

Iain Campbell reached out and squeezed her arm gently, as he had done so many times since the crash. He didn't look so good either. They were both hanging on by a thread.

'Hi Sammy!' he beamed as he walked into the kitchen. Sam's face lit up immediately, delighted to see his grandad.

Rosie tried not to notice her son's preference. There were too many other lacerations across her heart that needed to heal before she could tackle her problems with Sam. One day at a time, that was the best way.

'Everything ready to go?' Iain asked.

'I've gone through the checklist five times,' Rosie replied, more defensively than she'd intended. 'If those tossers from social care can't see that I'm better now, I'll scream. There are thousands of kids all over the country being neglected, yet they did that to me. I'd never harm Sammy; they should know that.'

She choked up, and Iain moved in to give her a hug.

'Nobody is questioning whether you're a good mother,' he said gently. 'They're just – well, it's just a precaution, while you fully recover. It's been a challenging couple of years. You're nearly there, Rosie. And it's this little one's second birthday on Saturday. That's something to look forward to, isn't it?'

Sam gave a squeal of delight. Rosie pulled herself away from her father and looked him in the face.

'Thanks, Dad. I mean it. Thank you. I don't know what I'd have done without you. Sometimes I feel like I'm going mad, but you're the reason I'm still here.'

'Don't say that, Rosie. You have so much to live for. You'll see. I know it's hard. I felt like that when your mother died. You'll get through it, Rosie; honestly, you will. Just keep going, you're nearly there.'

Rosie kissed him on the cheek and walked over to Sam. She knelt down by the highchair and forced a smile.

'See you later, Sam, be good for Grandad!'

She put on her coat, picked up her bag and gave them both a wave.

'Back by six,' she said. 'Unless the tube goes into melt-down, in which case, it may be days.'

Iain smiled, and she was pleased that she'd managed to squeeze out a flippant comment as they parted. It was the best she could do to put his mind at ease.

It may have been two years since she'd done this, but now she was dressed for work, her old bag packed for the day, it felt like it was only yesterday. If only it had been Liam sending her off to work.

It was only ten tube stops up the line from Lewisham, not bad for a London commute. She'd visit Liam at Green-wich, then hop back on the train and be at the office for a prompt nine o'clock start.

Haylee had sent her all the gossip since the buyout. A new HR guy had arrived, bringing brand new systems and processes for them all to learn. At least she was on a phased return, and they'd cut her some slack.

She was lucky that David Willis had been asked to stay with the firm for a year to see through the handover. He'd fought hard for her extended sick pay, while the new personnel department had been gunning for her from day one. If it wasn't for David, she'd have been out on her arse long before she could even contemplate a return to the workplace.

The tube seemed to have got worse. Last time she did this, it was busy but bearable at 7.15, but today she almost missed getting a seat. She still got so damn tired. Perhaps it was her medication.

Rosie got off at her stop and grabbed a coffee. At least she'd made one good decision, choosing to have Liam and Phoebe buried in the same cemetery as her mum. It worked well, three stops away and easy with the pushchair when she didn't have to navigate rush hours. She'd spent more time speaking to Liam than she should have. The key to recovery would lie in moving on, but she still needed him; she wasn't ready to do it all on her own just yet.

Rosie knew she shouldn't have used the first entrance the moment she walked through it, but she couldn't help herself; she had to force herself to see Phoebe. The tiny gravestones – fashioned into the forms of teddy bears and child-like angels – were surrounded with fresh flowers, soft toys and balloons.

What would her daughter have been like if she'd made it alive out of that wreckage instead of Sam? She still had no words for her dead child, the overwhelming surges of grief leaving her cold and numb. Rosie wanted to cry forever for the baby she'd lost, but there were no tears left.

She moved on, walking up the narrow asphalt path towards Liam's headstone. It wasn't right that father and daughter weren't buried together, but she'd been too out of her head on medication at the time to fight for it.

'Hi, Liam,' she whispered as she arrived at his headstone. Although the cemetery was vast, she could pinpoint his grave like a finely tuned GPS.

'Back to work today. It's been two years already – can you believe that? Wish me luck. It's going to be a difficult day.'

As she knelt down to adjust the flowers that she'd left there the previous weekend, Rosie realised that something wasn't quite right. It took her a moment to spot it. She'd had a small, circular plate added to the headstone, onto which a photo of Liam had been printed. They'd seen it done abroad, and it was something they'd both liked. It seemed to humanise the graves a little.

Liam's plate had been torn off the headstone. It took her

two minutes to locate it. It had been cast aside, thrown into a cluster of shrubs nearby.

'Bloody vandals,' Rosie cursed. But as she looked around at the other graves, she realised the only stone they appeared to have defaced was Liam's.

CHAPTER TWO

As Rosie ascended towards the thirteenth floor, she wondered if David still had the goatee. Apparently, he'd visited her in the psychiatric unit, but after a while, they'd all stopped coming. The nurses had said it didn't seem to be helping her. She never acknowledged them anyway, not in those first days.

She couldn't remember any of their visits and hoped that she hadn't done anything too embarrassing. Surely they'd forgive her; she was a sedated mess at Liam's funeral, so what did they expect?

It felt like no time at all since she'd made that journey. She'd worked at the company for over five years at the time of the accident and she was happy there, with her life set out before her. *They* had had their lives set out.

Rosie watched the numbers in the elevator as it headed towards her floor. It was always the same: floor thirteen was too high to take the stairs, but with the endless stopping and starting at that time of day, it could take up to ten minutes just to get through the front door of the office.

The lift doors slid open, and she walked out onto her

floor. So much had changed, even in that short time. The tech company opposite their offices had closed, and the unit was empty. As she looked through the windows into the office space, she saw a cubic capacity that would make any commercial lettings agent get excited. But with business rates so punishing, minimum wages increasing and worker rights ever-growing, it was becoming almost impossible to exploit a workforce like you could in the good old days.

And so, businesses like Cutting Edge Cyber Ltd had to close, no doubt reincarnating as online services either based in a cheaper home office set-up or recruiting remote staff in a region of the world where you could still employ graduates for peanuts.

At either side of Willis Supplies Ltd were two smaller concerns. WonderDeals Insurance brokers had always been there, at least ever since Rosie started working in the building. Insurance brokers were like cockroaches, and they still refused to die in spite of the competition from web-based providers. The first year she'd worked in the building, she insured her own vehicle there; later, she switched to the fast deals of the internet. Had she stayed with a broker, Rosie might have been a little more on top of the paperwork.

On the opposite side of the hallway was a second new business. This was some laser eye surgery establishment, sleek and hi-tech. What might have been more useful this high up was a sandwich shop, but they tended not to locate themselves in high-rise buildings in the middle of London's commercial centre.

She turned towards the entrance of Willis Supplies Ltd. The sign had been replaced by something that looked like it had been through the hands of several expensive brand managers. Silverline Supply Chains. That was her new employer. Even though she reported to David Willis – for the time being, at least – her salary slips had displayed the new logo for the past five months. With David still at the helm, it would just be the decor that had changed, surely?

Rosie pushed through the glass door and walked into reception. There was an immediate corporate feel, the air conditioning was immediately refreshing, and Haylee Madison looked like she was on the set of a US legal drama. Her eyes lit up when she saw who it was.

'Rosie!'

She jumped up from behind her desk, came out from her console and gave Rosie a big hug.

'David said you were back today. It's so good to see you. Are you okay now? You've been away so long.'

Rosie was prepared for this. Those first awkward moments. At least she only had Thursday and Friday to get through. Once all the initial nonsense was out of the way, it would all settle down, so long as she could make it through the first two days. That was her first target.

'David told me to send you straight in; he wants to be first to see you. I'll buzz him now, let him know you're on your way. Everything's changed since you left, Rosie. Hopefully, it'll all feel like normal now you're back.'

Rosie gave as much of a smile as she could muster and walked along the corridor towards David's office. The artwork had changed. David had a love of Jack Vettriano, claiming it was accessible and had a general appeal. Those beloved prints had now been removed in favour of what was obviously a corporate artwork service. There was a non-committal range of contemporary and classic artists, something for all tastes. Silverline Supply Chains were tinkering with David's successful formula; she wondered how that made him feel.

Rosie was grateful that she'd arrived during the morning

briefing. It allowed her to sneak into David's office under-cover, without being hijacked the moment she stepped through the door. A male voice was coming from the board-room along the corridor. She turned off towards David's office and moved her hand to knock on the door. She stopped mid-movement. David's nameplate was gone, replaced by a new, highly polished, brass fitting: *Edward Logan, HR Director.*

Rosie felt immediately disoriented. She ran through the office arrangements in her head. Where would David be now? He had to be in the corner office; it was the only other room that would suit somebody of his status within the company. That was the office he'd earmarked for her at Gina's leaving party.

She retraced her steps and found the corner office door; she'd walked straight past it on her way down. David's nameplate was still the original, plastic version; it was attached to the door with sticky tabs like it didn't intend on hanging around too long. She knocked at the door.

'Come in!'

David was out of his seat the moment he saw her walking through the door. He looked genuinely pleased to see her. She wished she could elicit the same response from her son.

'It's so good to have you back, Rosie,' David said, hugging her as if every bone in his body meant it. 'Take a seat; we've got a lot to catch up on.'

She sat down and admired the view of the city.

'So, how are you?' David asked, settling back into the high-backed leather seat, fortified behind his old, oak desk. The picture of his wife was no longer there. Another person taken by cancer. Had David moved on? Maybe that's what removing Maisie's photo had been all about.

'No family pictures allowed now,' David said as if reading her mind. 'Maisie has to remain a figment of my memory, in the office at least. Silverline Supply Chains doesn't care if you have loved ones – you're here to do a day's work, not get all teary-eyed about your deceased wife.'

Rosie looked at him, searching to see if this was a joke.

'I'm sorry, that's a bit dark for your first day,' he said with a grin. 'It's just that there have been a few changes around here. It's not the company I set up. My golden hand-cuffs come off in five months, then I'm gone. See, they haven't banned desk calendars yet!'

He held up a calendar on which his departure day was marked with a big, red circle.

'Anyway, enough of my gripes, it's your first day back. Welcome. I can't tell you how much everybody is looking forward to seeing you. There are a few new faces to get used to, of course. But enough of the old guard to make the place still feel like home.

'David, I want to thank you for what you did...'

He raised his hand to stop her.

'I won't hear anything about it,' he said. 'You know how much I value you as an employee. It's done now, and it was my pleasure.'

'I mean it, David,' she pushed. 'Two years of financial support from the company, even at a reduced rate. I couldn't have done it without your help. Thank you.'

'Well, Edward Logan soon put a stop to that, didn't he?' David grumbled. 'The man has left no stone unturned in his relentless search for efficiencies and cost savings. I'm sorry that we had to pull the rug out from beneath your feet. I just hope it wasn't too soon?'

David Willis was old-school. He'd built up the business as a young man, he and Maisie balancing a family with a fast-expanding supply chain company. Shipping containers were his thing. He'd started with one and was now responsible for hundreds of the things, moving to destinations all over the planet. Some feat for a man who had passed no exams and had spent his life at school being called thick. It was the term they used instead of learning difficulties in the sixties and seventies.

'Things have been a bit tough, as you'd expect,' Rosie said, trying her best to reassure him. If she was to hang onto her job, she'd need to give the impression of calm confidence and stability. A whiff of mental illness, and her phased return would swiftly turn into a sudden departure. It was a new rule book now; David was there for a restricted handover period, and once he'd gone, she'd be out on her arse if she didn't perform.

'Well, look, just a word to the wise,' David said in a conspiratorial tone. 'If you have any problems – and I mean anything, Rosie – talk to me first. It's pretty obvious they can't wait to show me the door, but while I have any influence here, I'll do my best to help you get your life back to normal. Don't hesitate, promise?'

'I promise,' Rosie replied. It would be impossible to have a better boss than David.

'Okay,' he continued. 'With that said, it's time to introduce you Edward Logan, our very delightful head of HR. Or as I affectionately like to call him, *The Terminator*.'

CHAPTER THREE

If vampires could go out in the day and feed on souls rather than blood, then Edward Logan would be one of them. His slicked-back hair, perfectly groomed beard, black suit and pointed shoes made him look like he'd just stepped off the set of a Hammer Horror movie. He out-vampired Christopher Lee.

Rosie shivered as she walked into Edward's office – David's old office. He kept it ridiculously cold in there, as if any burst of heat might awaken his heart and swiftly return the humanity to his host body. He was the perfect man for a job in HR.

The decor of the office reflected the man who occupied it. The paintings that hung on the walls were sparse and unenthusiastic, made up of spindly lines drawn with thin black and red ink. His desk was immaculately tidy, giving the impression of a man who had little to do until the excitement of new redundancies reared its head, or an opportunity arose to take down a member of staff through some performance review process or other HR device designed to squeeze out a member of staff from their much-needed job.

The only items on his desk when Rosie stepped in were an expensive ink pen and a camera.

'Ah, Rosie Taylor, staff number 347265L, welcome back to Silverline Supply Chains.'

He stood up calmly, got out from behind his desk and walked over to Rosie. She readied herself for an enthusiastic handshake, but Edward's hand felt limp and lifeless in hers.

She mangled her words for a few moments, then managed to release a fully formed sentence.

'It's good to be back here. You've certainly made some changes to David's office.'

'Now my office. As Director of HR, I take priority in the hierarchy. As I'm sure you're aware, David Willis will be leaving us soon.'

'He set up a remarkable business here; I'm sure his expertise is very much appreciated during the handover period.'

'His skills are all but obsolete, and I'm keen for him to move on now. We're good here; we know what we're doing.'

Rosie wasn't sure how to respond to that. Edward Logan could obviously take a conversational topic and kill it dead in its tracks, bludgeoning it for good measure. She changed the subject, moving it away from her former boss.

'Well, it's good to be back. I can't wait to get stuck in.'

'Yes. About that. Things have changed since you left. You've placed a considerable financial burden on the company during your absence. You start with no status here, and you'll have to earn that back. Truth be told, you've been a bit of a drain.'

He said this without emotion as if his humanity gauge wasn't troubled in the slightest by the words emerging from his mouth.

Rosie suppressed her panic and tried another tack. This

was one relationship that needed to go well if she was to continue to draw her much-needed salary.

'What made you get into HR?' she asked, trying to sound as cheery and interested as she could. She suspected it was his cold, unfeeling soul that had attracted him to the profession.

'I enjoy working with people and their problems...' Edward began.

Rosie nearly burst out laughing, assuming it was a joke. She hadn't done much laughing over the past two years. But Edward Logan was deadly serious.

'I believe that HR is a force for good, improving both company and employee. It allows me to give something back to the world.'

His face was straight, delivering his words without irony.

'I need to take a photo of you.'

'Now? Why?'

Edward nodded towards a montage of images to the side of his desk.

'Staff photographs. You'll need a pass. And I like to look at you all on my wall and imagine you hard at work. I stare at the images as a source of inspiration.'

That cold shiver was back again. Rosie had never met anybody like him.

'Stand against that plain wall, please,' he motioned with his hand and picked up the camera. 'It'll make a clean background for the image.'

Rosie did as she was told, finding a clear area between two of the prints on the walls. Edward held up the camera, pointing it towards her, twisting the lens to focus for the shot. He held the camera there for an uncomfortable amount of time, all the time his finger pressing on the button, the sound of the shutter confirming one photograph after another.

He moved in close, uncomfortably so, and pointed to a mole just above the neckline of her dress.

'You should get that mole checked out,' he said.

Rosie recoiled, baulking with revulsion as if an ugly insect had just swooped past her.

His breath was stale and rancid, as if he couldn't summon up enough propulsion for it to sustain life. Rosie felt immediately uncomfortable. She had her back against the wall with nowhere to go — the perfect positioning for a man from HR.

He moved away, returning the camera to his desk.

'I have sent an induction pack to your email address. You'll need to call IT to reset your password – your old account is still there. You seemed to spend a lot of time emailing your husband when you were here previously.'

He didn't finish the comment; it was just left there, half statement, half challenge.

Rosie didn't know how to answer.

'You've been looking through my emails?' was all she could manage. It was a more confrontational reply than she should have given, particularly after having benefited from the company sick pay scheme for much longer than normal. But it didn't trouble Edward in the slightest.

'Read the terms and conditions on the login screen. Your work emails are company property. As the HR Director, I have the right to read them. And I'd say you were spending too much time on personal emails during work time.'

Rosie felt her face turning bright red. He was right; she and Liam had messaged constantly. She got her work done; it was what everybody did, wasn't it? She felt a sense of excitement that there would be hundreds of old emails from Liam that she could read through. They would go back as far as when they'd met, perhaps even their first dates. That prospect was tinged with a sense of violation. There had been sexual chat in those emails – had Edward read those messages? She wanted to run out of the office with the shame and embarrassment of it all, but his icy stare held her there, like a rabbit frightened in headlights.

'I should take you to meet the other staff. Follow.'

Edward moved towards the door. She hated the way he spoke to her, both commanding and undermining. Was this some kind of first-day power play?

The company was divided up into a number of offices. Haylee Madison on the reception desk was always the first to greet a potential customer and place them in the comfortable waiting area. A length of corridor, with doors off to the meeting rooms, the board room and the staff kitchen, led to the office area which was divided into departments. Sales, administration, accounts – that was it. Plus, of course, the newly formed HR department, consisting only of Edward, as far as Rosie could tell.

'Why is the sales office empty?' Rosie asked as they passed the space where old workmates like Terry Fincham and Phil Herring usually resided.

'Too much time chatting on the phones. Sales personnel should be out in the field, talking to new prospects, not wasting time on chit-chat. I introduced a new system whereby sales staff are not permitted into the office until they can evidence ten personal contacts in a day.'

Rosie thought back to the laughs she'd had in that office. It was the place where political correctness had gone to die, and Terry Fincham managed to walk that very fine line between being wholly inappropriate yet hilariously funny.

She wondered how he was coping with their new HR director.

The next office was accounts, where Rosie sensed discomfort from Edward Logan.

'That's where the accounts team are based, but you know that already,' he said, preparing to do a fly-past.

A ferocious sounding Glaswegian voice bellowed out from within the room.

'Rosie Taylor!'

'Neil Jennings!' she replied.

Despite giving out a visible air of respectability with his grey, well-cropped hair and light grey suit, Neil Jennings had an inner rage and power, like a bomb set on a hairpin trigger. Perhaps he was driven to over-compensate for his lack of height. But with Rosie, he was always charming. Neil moved in and held his arms out.

'Is it still permissible to give a lassie a wee hug?' he sneered at Edward. 'I would'na want ta get in trouble with the HR guy!'

Rosie moved towards Neil; she'd always liked the man, in spite of everybody else being wary of him. Seeing familiar faces made it seem like the last two years had never happened. If only Liam could be waiting at home for her when she returned in the evenings.

'Watch that tosser,' Neil mumbled in her ear as they embraced, 'He's a dangerous wee shite.'

For the first time since she'd met him, Rosie sensed discomfort in Edward Logan.

'He's scared of me,' Neil chuckled. 'I like to keep the wanker on his toes.'

Neil gave Rosie a conspiratorial wink, and they pulled away from each other.

'No saliva exchanged and definitely no erection,' Neil

spat out his words at Edward with contempt. 'If ya'd like me to, I'm happy to fill out a full report?'

Edward appeared not to know how to react. Neil's machine-gun delivery placed him on the ropes. At least Edward wasn't unassailable. That gave Rosie some small comfort. She greeted the accounts team, then followed Edward's lead to move on.

Annabelle Reece-Norton headed up the administration office. All the chatter stopped immediately when they entered.

'Hello Annabelle. It's quiet in here,' Rosie said, shattering the silence.

As Annabelle stood up immediately to greet her, the other members of staff began to talk, welcoming Rosie back.

'Please get back to your work and stop wasting salaried time on idle chit-chat!'

Edward hushed the room instantly. Heads went down as the entire office returned to work, like Victorian factory workers following the owner's commands.

'Let's speak later,' Annabelle whispered. 'I'll fill you in with what's going on around here.'

Edward Logan's presence had the effect of a malevolent spectre, immediately dulling any spark of life and leaving behind a bitter, resentful room.

'And this is where you'll be based,' Edward told her as they walked down the corridor. 'I don't subscribe to personal offices, unless a role requires it, such as my own in HR. However, until I rearrange the company structure, you get this office. David told me he'd promised you the corner office before you left on maternity leave. I don't believe in allocating offices in order to boost the status of staff members. I'd rather we stored paperwork in that room when he's gone. This is your office; I'll leave you to phone IT and get your computer sorted out. Please make a list of any stationery that you take from the stock room, sign and date it and leave it in my in-tray.'

He didn't wait for a response or ask if Rosie had any questions. He simply abandoned her outside her office door. The signage had not been changed, and it still read *Filing*.

Rosie opened the door and walked inside. She'd barely noticed this room in the past. Previously it had been used by the admin team. She switched on the light. There was no window to provide any natural illumination. A row of filing cabinets lined the far wall, and in the middle was a polished desk which looked like it had just been brought up from the basement. It was old-fashioned but perfectly serviceable. The accompanying office chair appeared to have seen better days, and it was wearing badly at its padded edges.

Rosie sat down on the chair.

'I can do this. I can do this,' she repeated in her head.

Her hand reached to the top drawer and opened it. It was empty.

She closed it up and reached down for the lower drawer, opening it up.

That's when she began to scream.

CHAPTER FOUR

'What is it, Rosie?'

Annabelle was first on the scene.

'There's a dead rat in my drawer!' Rosie screamed, backed up against the filing cabinets, repulsed by what she'd seen.

'Oh no, are you sure it's dead?' Annabelle asked, retreating towards the door.

'It's dead, but it's not an old one, it looks like it only just died.'

A dark-haired man walked into the room, followed by a young girl, who appeared to be of school age. Rosie didn't recognise either of them. The man walked up to the drawer, opened it up and peered inside.

'Damn, that's some size for a rat,' he said. 'It's dead. It won't hurt you,' he said, in a reassuring tone. 'I'm James – James Bygraves. I'm a temp here. Pleased to meet you.'

He held out his hand, and Rosie became aware that she'd been cowering in the corner.

'You're certain it's dead?' she asked.

'Definitely.'

He had a pleasant smile, instantly charming and warm. Rosie shook his hand.

'MacKenzie, how about you get Rosie a coffee while I dispose of the rat?'

Rosie surmised MacKenzie was the young girl, who now nodded at James and left the room. She was young, with aggressively shaved hair at the sides of her head and dyed long, pink locks flowing from the top. Her nose and lip were pierced, and she had heavy eye make-up and sculpted eyebrows. Rosie wondered who she was. She seemed familiar in some vague way. But she was very young to be working there. Edward had obviously skimped on his office tour.

'Why don't you take a seat in the meeting room across the corridor? I'll get rid of this and disinfect the drawer for you.'

'Thank you, that's really kind of you.'

Rosie walked over to the meeting room, trying to calm herself. Not only had Edward Logan's greeting unsettled her and made her feel like she was a temporary presence, but this rat had also shaken her nerves. She was constantly on edge as it was: her hands were shaking, and she was struggling to steady her voice. Rosie fought to hide the signs. She mustn't give any indication of how close she was to collapsing. This job was vital; she was desperate for the money.

The quiet of the meeting room was just what she needed. She sat in silence for ten minutes, taking slow, deep breaths and staring out of the window. Her office was the only one in that cluster of rooms which relied on artificial light. It seemed remarkable that it should be designated as her workspace; it had more in common with a solitary confinement cell.

'All clear!'

James entered the room, his friendly smile apparently a permanent fixture. Rosie noticed he was good-looking in a well-groomed, non-macho kind of way. It was a long time since she'd even noticed a man's appearance.

'Don't worry, I've disinfected your desk and washed my hands three times with antiseptic hand wash. I'm clean enough to perform an operation, though I don't recommend it – I can barely wire a plug. Sorry about that. It's one hell of a way to come back to work!'

Rosie took his hand and shook it. It was soft to the touch; he'd never done a day's manual work in his life, that was for sure. Her dad's hands were calloused and rough after years of physical labour. Liam's had been like James'; they were a lucky generation of men.

'Who was the girl?' Rosie asked, intrigued by the striking teenager.

'That's MacKenzie,' James answered. 'MacKenzie Devereux. She's an intern here. Did she ever bring you that coffee?'

'No,' Rosie replied. 'Now you mention it, the coffee never arrived.'

'Sorry about that; she gets easily distracted. You know what teenagers are like – attention spans like gnats, glued to their mobile phones. I work in admin, by the way - I'm in between jobs. I saw you earlier, but I don't think you noticed me?'

'No, no, I'm sorry, I didn't. It's all pretty overwhelming, to be honest with you. So many faces, and so much to catch up with. I hardly know where to begin.'

'Well, your office is now 100% clear of rats. I'd better get back to work; I don't want Edward breathing down my neck with his fifteen-minute rule!'

'What's the fifteen-minute rule?'

'Edward insists on you staying on at work for an extra fifteen minutes if he catches you wasting time. It's why the office is so quiet when he's around. Everybody wants to escape the moment the clock strikes five. We're like a bunch of corporate Cinderellas, all desperate to get away before the chimes of the clock.'

He laughed at his own quip.

'You're kidding, aren't you?' Rosie asked.

'No joke,' James said. 'Beware the reaper's scythe, Edward Logan is out to get you!'

He smiled and left the meeting room.

Every bone in Rosie's body was telling her that things weren't right here, but she had no plan for what to do. How could a workplace become so dysfunctional so fast?

She resolved to keep her head down and get on with it. She had to claw back the arrears on the mortgage and pay off the credit card debt. Sam seemed to be getting bigger by the week and was constantly growing out of his clothes. And if the social workers were going to leave her alone, she'd have to convince them that she was stable now – even if she knew that she wasn't. Rosie realised she'd have to suck it up, in spite of the uneasy feeling in the pit of her stomach from the moment she'd met Edward Logan.

She spent the remainder of the morning stocking her drawers and organising her work area. After what seemed an interminable amount of time hanging on the end of a phone line, she also got her computer login restored.

'All my old emails are gone,' she said to the tech-guy who had patiently worked through everything with her.

'Yeah, we got authorisation to ground zero your account.'

'Who from?' Rosie asked. She knew the answer.

'The initials are EL. It was only done this week. Everything was archived and moved over to HR. That's unusual, but they're allowed to do it under the T&Cs. You should read them sometime. Nothing you do on your work PC is private.'

At last lunchtime arrived and she left the office with a massive sense of relief. She'd never felt that way before; her time at Willis Supplies Ltd had always been happy. She was glad to see the food truck was still stationed in the small square opposite the office block, feeding the workers from the surrounding high-rise buildings. She'd intended to bring sandwiches to save money, but with Sam creating such a fuss, things hadn't worked out that way.

Rosie took out her mobile phone and called her dad. She was relieved when he figured out how to answer it after nine rings.

'Everything's fine, Rosie – me and Sam are having a lovely day. In fact, we're at the park right now. I can't get him off this swing.'

She longed for a time when she could share her dad's easy relationship with her son. She was always so tense, as if she resented Sam for surviving over Phoebe. Whatever he did, she framed him as a bully, as if he'd pushed his sister aside and dared to survive the accident. She knew she was being ridiculous. It was the luck of the draw, but that's how her mind worked since the crash. Sam was an innocent two-year-old, and he'd got lucky – the surgeons had got to him first. An emergency caesarean with an unconscious mother. She was lucky they'd got one child out alive.

As Rosie tucked into her baked potato, she was aware of somebody approaching. She looked up to see Haylee, a polystyrene container packed with food in her hand.

'Hey, Rosie. How's it going?' She sat at Rosie's side.

'Hi Haylee. It feels like a long time since you and I did this. I've got beans with my potato – it's the cheapest option. I should really be eating sandwiches.'

'The place has changed, hasn't it?' Haylee said, out of the blue. 'You must see it, Rosie – it's not just me, is it?'

Rosie rested her plastic fork in the polystyrene tray.

'It's different, that's for sure,' she replied. 'This Edward Logan guy, he's a bit of an odd one, isn't he?'

'He scares everybody,' Haylee said. Rosie noticed that she was struggling to hold back tears.

'He keeps telling us how expensive we are and that David was over-paying us. He even makes a big thing about me going on my lunch break and monitors how long we're out of the office. Can you believe that? You know, he actually keeps a note if we're back just a few minutes late.'

'I guess I don't know him well enough yet,' Rosie said, thinking about the way he'd remarked on her mole. It made her feel a little sick just thinking about it.

'He calls me at home, too. In the evenings and at weekends. He even came to my house once.'

'Edward did? Surely not?'

'Yes, seriously. He keeps calling with trivial questions about things that happened during the workday. He calls at all times of the night. How do you stop him? He has to have our personal information because he's the HR guy. It's really getting to me Rosie – I'm thinking about leaving. But that bastard manages the references too, so I have to stay on the right side of him.'

Rosie had never seen Haylee like this before, unburdening herself; she hadn't even started eating her own baked potato. Her eyes were red as she fought back the tears.

'I'm sorry,' Haylee said, touching Rosie's arm. 'Here I

am, sounding off about my own problems, and I haven't even caught up with you properly yet.'

'It's okay,' Rosie replied, picking up her fork again. 'Don't leave just yet, Haylee – I've only just got back. It'll be alright, just like the old times, you'll see. Everything's going to be totally fine.'

Even as she said the words, Rosie wasn't entirely convinced if it was Haylee she was trying to persuade, or herself.

CHAPTER FIVE

Rosie heard the two sales guys before she saw them. She assumed they must have met their quotas for the day and they were back in the office now, no doubt after their customary boozy lunch. She'd been gone for two years. How much damage must Phil and Terry have inflicted on their livers in that time?

She didn't think for one moment that the pair of them were racist, sexist, genderist, veganist or whatever other -ists existed in twenty-first century Britain. But they could make everybody roar with laughter. They sailed as close to the wind as was humanly possible without losing their jobs. David Willis had tried his luck in taming them once or twice, but Terry and Phil had been the first two sales employees in the business, and they'd exceeded their targets year-in, year-out. They were part of the furniture. But, as Rosie had already seen for herself, the furniture had been changed already since she'd been gone.

There was a knock at Rosie's door. She began to answer, but Terry was already in the room, appearing to ignore her, pulling his trousers down and pretending to go to the toilet.

'Phil! Phil! There's a lady in the gents' toilet! Get her out of here.'

Phil entered the room, cackling away.

'Fancy putting you in this shit-hole!' he said. 'Pull your trousers up mate. You'll get caught by off-his-heady-Eddy.'

Terry pulled up his trousers and buckled his belt.

'We've got to behave these days.' Terry smiled at Rosie, walking over and giving her a hug. 'Normally I'd touch you inappropriately, but I'd lose my job.'

Rosie laughed. She knew that he didn't mean it and would never do it; it was just how they were, a double act.

Phil moved to the far wall.

'You know there's a window in this room, don't you? Give me a hand Tez. Look, here it is – it's just a bit of hardboard glued over the frame.'

They were like a whirlwind, the two of them in perfect harmony, moving over towards a board which Rosie had assumed was a place to pin memos and a calendar. Their fingers worked away at it until they managed to pull it away from its fixing. Light flooded into the small office, nourishing her after two hours illuminated only by a strip light and a desk lamp.

'I would never have known that was there. I might have died in here,' Rosie said.

Terry and Phil lowered the board and moved it behind the filing cabinets.

'You'll need to pay for that damage.'

Edward was at the door, peering in.

'Look what you've done to the paintwork. And look at the state of the glass. I'll be invoicing you for the damage.'

He walked off as abruptly as he'd arrived.

'And you know where you can stick your invoice, don't

you?' Terry snarled, at a suitable level of volume that it wouldn't be heard by Edward.

'Fucking tosser!' Phil said. 'I've worked here all my life, and I've never wanted to punch a man in the face as much as I want to punch Edward Logan. I haven't got a degree or any qualifications, but if that's what an education does for you, I'm glad I left school at sixteen.'

'You're a bit generous with your timescales there, aren't you mate?' Terry queried.

'Alright, yeah, I left at fifteen. But that was unofficial. Officially I left at sixteen, so my ma could still claim the family allowance for me.'

The two men laughed, a couple of amateur comedians, bouncing off each other constantly.

'Are you coming out for drinks tomorrow?' Terry asked. 'I know you've got the baby now, but you'll still come along for the TGI Friday piss-up won't you?'

'Shhh!' Phil warned. 'Make sure Logan's not around.'

Rosie looked from Terry to Phil and back to Terry.

'We've managed to keep it a secret from him for almost half a year,' Terry began. 'He thinks we all go home at five o'clock on a Friday. But we coordinate it by a WhatsApp group. We all leave one by one, then meet up around the corner. The prick still doesn't know we do it.'

Rosie cast her mind back to the Friday ritual. Once upon a time, they'd make an evening of it, and Liam would join her. She hadn't drunk in two years. How could she, after the crash? And she had to think of her drugs too. The first rule of anti-depressants and anxiety pharmaceuticals was no alcohol.

'I'd love to come along,' she replied, 'but no late-night booze ups or pub grub. Number one: I can't really afford it, and number two: my dad is looking after Sam. I'll join you for a soft drink, but I can't stay late.'

The sun was pouring in through the window of her office. Rosie couldn't believe it was the same space. There was an amazing view out over the commercial district, making her feel like a mole that had just broken through the surface of the soil.

David popped into the room.

'I'd forgotten that the window was covered up; we did that years ago. Blimey, it looks far better in here. We did it to protect all the paperwork from the sun. It gets wonderful light in this room. That's a lot better. I felt terrible when Edward told me he was putting you in here, Rosie. I know I promised you the office that I'm in, but our friend in HR put a stop to that. He outranks me under this new arrangement. I'm just here until my brains are picked clean, then I'll be on my way.'

'You can't get Mike up here to sort that paintwork out, can you?' Phil asked. 'The Loganator is threatening to dock it from our pay. He'll touch it up for us, won't he?'

David moved fully into the room, so he couldn't be heard.

'Strictly speaking, I need to put a form in for it these days. But Mike owes me a favour. I'll call him now, see if he'll pop up and sort it out. It'll only take ten minutes to fix; it takes longer than that to fill out Edward's form.'

David phoned down to the caretaker's office and gave him the update on the paintwork situation. While he was speaking, Rosie whispered to Phil.

'Is that the same guy who used to work here two years ago? Old Mikey, the man who never retires?'

'That's him,' Terry replied, not giving Phil time to respond. 'He's still here. The man refuses to stop working.'

Rosie gave David a signal, indicating that she wanted him to hand over the phone before he finished with Mike. He passed it over to her, and she resumed the call.

'Hi Mike, it's Rosie – Rosie Taylor. I don't know if you remember me?'

He did. That surprised her; they'd only ever exchanged pleasantries.

'Did you bring the desk up from the basement for the filing cabinet office? You know the one, don't you? Yes. There was a rat in the bottom drawer. You don't need to get some traps down there, do you?'

The unsettled feeling that had been sitting uncomfortably in her stomach all day worsened the moment Mike gave his answer.

He'd checked and cleaned the drawers himself before leaving the room. They were completely empty; he was certain of it. If there was a dead rat in that drawer, it had to have got there after he'd left the room.

CHAPTER SIX

The smell of fresh paint reminded Rosie of her time at Trinity Heights Psychiatric Hospital. As she'd emerged from her drugged stupor and slowly returned to the land of the sentient, it had been one of the first things she noticed.

It turned out that wasn't such a good thing in a psychiatric unit. One of the long-term patients there – a young girl called Tamsin – would crack her head against the pale blue walls whenever she became distressed. The blood from her forehead was so hard to wash off that it was easier to wipe it, let it dry and then paint over it. Vera had told her that during one of their talks. Lovely Vera, the woman who'd returned her to the world of the living.

Rosie would often wonder just how bad she was if she was in the same ward as Tamsin. It terrified her, sitting in that office, thinking about how precarious life could be. How she could go from being a city high-flyer to a complete mental wreck, and then back to the day job, after everything that had happened to her? She wasn't out of the woods yet, and she knew it.

She'd put on a brave face for the social workers, effective enough to have secured shared custody of Sam with her father. What a win that had been, as she began the long, slow climb back from the mental abyss. She'd moved through the psychiatric hospital from being forcibly sectioned, to voluntarily committing herself, progressing to being a day patient and finally going back to the house to live with her father under the same roof. And for two months now, she'd lived there alone, still using a lower dosage of drugs, looking after Sam on her own and reclaiming her former life, day by hard-won day.

For a moment, as she looked out of her office window, she felt proud of herself. It was two years after those terrible events, yet here she was, still alive, still fighting, salvaging the ruined remains of her former life.

Rosie had been running through Edward's newly updated induction manual since Mike had re-painted the window surround. She'd swiftly tired of it and chose instead to be distracted by the wonderful office view over London.

'Hiya!'

Rosie was shaken out of her daydreaming by an unfamiliar voice. It was the girl who was meant to have brought her coffee after her shock with the rat. If this was it arriving now, she was a bit late.

'You're Rosie then, the one who was in the mental unit?'

That took Rosie aback. Was that how they'd been speaking about her while she was absent?

The girl was young – eighteen or nineteen maybe – and she was chewing gum. Her trousers and top were figure-hugging, and she was displaying much more cleavage that was appropriate in any workplace. Her nails were immaculately painted with a bright, red varnish and her eyebrows were sculpted to within an inch of their life. She was astounded that Edward permitted such a colourful and shocking hairstyle. Rosie knew better than to judge her by appearance alone.

'You must be the apprentice?' Rosie asked, choosing to ignore the bluntness of the introduction.

'Yeah, I'm Mackenzie. I need to get into those filing cabinets behind your desk.'

She held up a handful of files and raised her eyebrows, indicating to Rosie that she'd need to get out of the way to let her past.

'Delighted to meet you, Mackenzie. It's about time we started taking on apprentices here – I'm surprised we left it so long.'

Rosie held out her hand, expecting her gesture to be reciprocated. Instead, Mackenzie looked at it like it was consumed with the pox, shrugged and started moving towards the filing cabinets. Rosie retracted her hand; maybe youngsters didn't bother with such workplace pleasantries any more. She felt old.

Mackenzie moved over to the filing cabinets and began to flick through the hanging files, seeking the correct location for her folders.

'So, what do you think about the blokes around here? A bit old for my liking – only a couple of them are fit.'

Thankfully Mackenzie's back was facing Rosie, because she could feel her face turning red at the directness of the question. She was torn between giving some gentle guidance about how to behave in the workplace and telling the girl off. However, on day one at work after a two-year absence, which had caused the new HR department a great deal of consternation, Rosie decided to use evasion tactics as her preferred strategy.

'Doesn't it look better in here with that hardboard taken

off the window? Goodness knows who put it there in the first place. I'm certain this room was cut off from the light when I last worked here. What a waste – just look at that view of the commercial district.'

Mackenzie was having none of it.

'So, what's it like having a dead husband?' she asked.

Rosie was stuck for words. She decided to change tack. Mackenzie seemed to appreciate straight-talking.

'It's pretty damn horrible, to tell you the truth.'

'I bet it is. My mate's dad died last year; it was awful. He was really bummed out for ages. I feel sorry for you.'

'That's nice of you to say, Mackenzie, thank you.'

She wondered for one moment if Mackenzie just had an unfortunate way with words.

'You've got a kid, haven't you?' she continued.

'You seem to know a lot about me,' Rosie remarked.

'Yup,' she replied, as if Rosie ought to have known that all along. 'It's all on Google,' she added.

'What's on Google?' Rosie asked. 'I'm only on Facebook and LinkedIn. Oh, and WhatsApp now—'

She finished her sentence abruptly, not certain if the office apprentice was in on the Friday drinks or not. She didn't want to be the one to let the cat out of the bag if it was supposed to be a secret after-work drinking club.

'You can read all about it,' Mackenzie replied. 'About your hubby Liam, about the kid that died. It's all there. And how he was over the limit when he crashed the car—'

'Okay, that's enough!' Rosie said. 'I've come here to get away from that and put the past behind me. I'd appreciate it if you didn't talk to me about it again.'

She felt the burning sense of frustration surging through her once again. Her hand reached out for her bag to find a pill, but she stopped herself; she'd have to make sure none of her work colleagues spotted her taking medication. It had been some time since she'd felt that combination of loss for Liam and a raging fury that he'd been over the drink-drive limit. How could he have been so damn stupid?

'Whatever,' Mackenzie answered, like it was water off a duck's back. 'I didn't mean anything by it. Shit happens sometimes. There's no point wetting your panties over it.'

She continued with her filing in silence. Rosie was anxious that their first interaction didn't end like that. She had to rekindle old friendships and nurture new ones if this was going to work out for her. It had to go well, or she was in financial trouble.

'So, have you finished school, Mackenzie, or is this some sort of placement?'

'I'm finished with school,' she replied, as if the previous conversation had never taken place. 'I wasn't doing anything for a little while. In fact I never really finished school, it just kind of ended. Anyhow, my mam told me I had to do something, or I was out on my arse. So I went for some shitty jobs, and I couldn't get any. Then David took me on. He told me he couldn't give me proper work, but he'd make me an apprentice while I got some skills. And here I am.'

Mackenzie took the gum out of her mouth and just for a moment, Rosie saw that she was actually considering sticking it under her newly delivered desk, like an involuntary action that hadn't yet been unlearned from school. Instead, she hesitated, then flicked it directly and with startling accuracy into Rosie's bin.

'Good shot!' Rosie replied. She couldn't come up with any better response than that.

'That's what I said to James Bygraves when we came in

here for a secret snog. It used to be a great place to sneak off to when that window was covered, and before they took it over for your office. What do you think of James? I think he's the hottest guy in this office, don't you?'

CHAPTER SEVEN

'You've been a right prick, David, you really have!'

It was five o'clock and Rosie was delighted to have made it through the first day. But the sound of Neil and David having some fallout about the accounts handover was making her stomach churn. She had to pass David's office to get to reception, but she wanted to give this verbal brawl a wide berth.

'They had their chance to do due diligence, and it's not as if you didn't spend enough time with their accounts team.'

David's voice was patient and measured. But Neil sounded like he was on the verge of tearing out his superior's throat and feeding it to his demon children. Rosie knew him of old; the Glaswegian accent made his bark sound far worse than his bite.

She needed to make a dash for the tube, knowing it would rise to a crescendo of rushing workers by half-five. The last thing she needed was to be crammed into the carriages, trapped in a prison of bad breath, body odour and uncomfortable proximity.

Rosie decided to make a run for it. The two men sounded so embroiled by their conversation; they were unlikely to notice her sneaking past David's door. But that wasn't her only problem as it turned out.

'Going home already?'

It was Edward. His office door was wide open, and he was on the prowl.

Rosie stopped and considered her response. It had been difficult enough finding a constructive way into conversation with Mackenzie. She was an odd girl, obsessed with unusual topics, but maybe Rosie was just getting old. She had a kind heart though, and she'd offered to babysit Sam if Rosie ever wanted to go out *on a Tinder date or something like that*. The thought was there, at least. Rosie decided she'd pass on that for the time being. She really didn't know what to make of the office apprentice just yet, she was an unusual cocktail of clumsy friendliness and awkward over-sharing.

'Well, it is five o'clock, and the staff manual does have that noted as the end of the working day. See, I've been reading the information you gave me!'

She said it in as cheery and non-confrontational a way as she could manage.

'Hmm,' Edward replied. 'That's there as a guide rather than a rule.'

It looked pretty much like a rule to Rosie, but she wasn't going to quibble; she had a tube train to catch.

'I'll be here until at least seven o'clock doing the company's work.'

More fool you, she thought.

'Well, as you'll know from David, I have to get back home to relieve my dad from child-minding duties. He's been looking after Sam all day and he's supposed to be retired. I don't want to take advantage of his good nature.'

'Maybe you need to reconsider your childcare options?' Edward suggested.

'The staff book says that Silverline Supply Chains is a family-friendly work environment,' Rosie ventured. 'I do hope that's not just paying lip-service to the idea?'

Edward didn't miss a beat.

'As I said, these are just guidelines. Don't think of the staff handbook as a legal document. It's more of a wish list, an aspiration. I like to think that if people are happy enough to draw a salary from the company, they'll be just as content to put in a full day's work.'

Rosie took some long breaths to calm herself down. It wouldn't be the smartest idea to get into a fight with the HR guy on her first day in the office.

'I've taken my lead from how David used to run the office. I'm sure it won't take me long to get a feel for how things work around here now,' she said, in a neutral tone.

'David isn't in charge any more. It's no longer his company. He's serving out his agreed handover period; then he's out of here. You might say I make the rules now,' Edward continued, sharp and without emotion.

His words hung there for a moment, while Rosie considered what response she might give. Instead of coming up with something smart or witty, she just bungled her way out of it.

'Well, I'd best be going. I've noted what you said about working hours – thanks for the heads-up. Cheerio!'

She gave a wave and shot along the corridor. Neil and David were still shouting at each other. She wondered if she'd entered some parallel universe, the easy-going tone in the building having vanished in the two years since she'd been away. She couldn't put her finger on it; everybody seemed on edge, as if expecting a big fight to kick off at any moment. It sounded like Neil and David were having theirs already.

'As the top guy in the organisation, you're supposed to have a grasp of all this, David.'

'You've been here long enough to know that I rely on people like you for things like that.'

Rosie paused at the side of the door, waiting for one of them to speak, then darted across the opening as fast as she could manage. She made a mess of it, dropping her phone onto the floor. Both men stopped and looked at her. Rosie glanced at them, embarrassed at having been caught.

'See you tomorrow,' she said, forcing a smile.

David and Neil cooled for a moment, aware for the first time that their disagreement was being heard throughout the building.

'I'm sorry I haven't caught up with you properly today, Rosie,' David began, with a look of embarrassment. 'I promise I'll make time tomorrow. Just call in to my office whenever you want.'

'Will do,' she replied, desperate to be on her way.

'See you later, Rosie.' Neil said, more gently. 'Sorry you had to hear that on your first day back in the office. Things have changed around here since you were away. And not for the best.'

'No problem, Neil. Bye!'

She gave a wave and darted towards reception. Haylee had gone already, like a whippet out of a trap, leaving the phones on night service. She was the lucky one – she could make her escape straight out of the front door, so nobody ever saw her go. So unlike before, when she called by the other offices and have a chat before leaving, Rosie recalled.

James Bygraves was sitting on one of the comfortable chairs in the reception area. He was reading a brochure, but didn't look engaged, as if simply passing the time.

'Hi, James,' Rosie began, 'Have you got a long journey home?'

Rosie had done the maths in her head. She'd missed that crucial time to beat the rush hour crush. She figured she may as well get to know another one of her work colleagues, now she was committed to cattle-truck travel.

'Hi Rosie,' he replied, seemingly pleased to be able to place the bland brochure back onto the coffee table and do something more interesting. 'How was your first day?'

'Unusual,' Rosie replied. It was the only way she could describe it.

'Hah – you can say that again. I see all sorts of workplace cultures in my temp work. This one is pretty unique.'

'It never used to be that way,' Rosie said. 'Once upon a time, you'd have heard howls of laughter coming from these offices at this time of day. It used to oil the wheels well – most of us rubbed along nicely.'

'Well, you'll be treated to a day of full-on Edward soon,' James smiled.

'Oh yes, what's happening?'

'You know about the away day?' he asked.

'No, when's that?'

Nobody had mentioned an away day.

'Next Saturday, on Valentine's Day of all days.'

'You're kidding?' she asked. 'Is it compulsory? Where is it?'

'Yes, it's compulsory. And it's somewhere in Kent. Edward didn't even see fit to leave us in London.'

'Bloody hell,' Rosie cussed, 'I've only just got here, and they're messing around with my childcare days. You're certain it's not this Saturday? I have something on this weekend.'

'No, next Saturday and Sunday, and you can have one day off in lieu. Still, it's of no concern to me this year. It'll take my mind off things on Valentine's Day. This time last year, I was in a relationship. This year, I'm all on my own. I'll be grateful for the distraction, I reckon.'

He made a good point. He wasn't the only one going home to a house with no adult company. Rosie recalled what Mackenzie had told her about James earlier on that day. He didn't seem like the kind of man to behave like that. She wondered if their apprentice was making things up. And if so, what would make her do such a thing?

CHAPTER EIGHT

Rosie had decided to get some shopping in at the Express store on the way over to the tube, and James had come with her. Her father had texted that he and Sam weren't back from their adventures yet, so she didn't feel guilty about getting home a little later. She was more tired than she'd expected too, and the thought of throwing a ready-made meal into the microwave was tempting.

James had taken it in his stride when she'd told him she had a baby. That was a good start, at least. He was her kind of age too, thirty to thirty-five she reckoned. Too old for a youngster like Mackenzie, surely?

She'd gently probed a bit, trying to see if he would spill the beans about the claims that Mackenzie had made. It just didn't sit right. Besides, James was a temp. He'd be sacked if he got caught having inappropriate relations with the apprentice in the filing room. She didn't need to read Edward's boring handbook to know that much. Mackenzie would be dismissed too.

As she sat on the sofa, the lights dimmed, Sam asleep upstairs in his bedroom and her father now fed, watered and on his way home, Rosie thought about what James had told her. Thank God her dad was clear to provide child cover the following weekend. It was Sam's birthday on Sunday, the most difficult day of the year for Rosie. She'd be celebrating one birth while mourning one stillborn child and a dead, over the drink-drive limit husband.

It would be the first year she'd tackled it free of tranquilisers. The year before, she'd been lying in a psychiatric hospital in a drug-induced stupor. The year before that, surgeons had been fighting to save her life and the life of her unborn babies. Two years after, almost to the day, she was expected to smile sweetly – alongside Sam's young friend and his mother – and help to blow out the candles on a sickly birthday cake with a picture of Peppa Pig iced on it.

At least Sam had done the decent thing and managed to hang on until after midnight. The one saving grace about the entire sorry episode was that Liam and Phoebe had died before the stroke of midnight, meaning that Sam's birthday was on a different day.

Vera had coached her through that.

'Separate the days,' she'd advised. 'Make the first day a day of mourning. Howl at the moon, stomp, scream, shout – do whatever you have to in order to grieve over Phoebe and Liam. But when that clock strikes midnight, remember it's a brand new day. The next day brought a new life into the world. Celebrate that, rejoice that Sam is alive, and embrace the life that you have before you. Your life didn't end in that crash either, Rosie. In many ways, it was only just getting started.'

Vera was right. She usually was. She must have seen so many depressed and desperate people in her line of work that she probably had an answer for everything. But it worked for Rosie. It helped her to navigate a way through it.

On Saturday, she would tend the graves with Sam in his pushchair, leave flowers, buy Phoebe a new soft toy and do a lot of crying. On Sunday, Leone would come round with Owen, and they'd stuff themselves with crisps and cake, watch two toddlers snatching toys from each other and no doubt sneak in a glass of wine. It was worth the risk of mixing the alcohol with her drugs – if she couldn't celebrate one day of the year, what else was there left for her?

At the Express store, James had told her that Edward called at his house sometimes. He would arrive during an evening or weekend and ask him something trivial about work. James warned her to watch out for it.

'One Saturday morning, it was just past nine o'clock, and Edward turned up. I didn't know what to say. He wanted to ask me about something I'd been working on that week.'

'Couldn't it have waited until Monday?' Rosie asked.

'That's what I said,' James replied. 'I was really cross with him, but I didn't have anything else lined up work-wise, so I couldn't tell him to piss off. I wanted to, that's for sure.'

It had unsettled Rosie once again. What was Edward doing calling on staff outside of work hours? David Willis had never needed to do that in all the time she'd worked there previously. It was just one more thing that seemed to be messed up at the firm. Most of it tracked back to Edward. He was a strange man.

Rosie picked up her phone. It was her lifeline, with her father looking after Sam so much. She was so exhausted that she couldn't even be bothered to turn on the TV. Instead, she idly scrolled through her Facebook posts, barely absorbing the content and looking at the pictures and videos to pass the time before heading for bed.

A message request appeared on her screen from James Bygraves. She had to accept the request to see the message. James hadn't completed his profile. There was no photograph and nothing to identify him other than the name. It made sense that he might want to connect after their genial chat that evening. She hadn't made many Facebook friends in the psychiatric unit. In fact, she hadn't received a new friend request for some time.

Rosie accepted the message request and looked to see what James was sending. She recoiled instantly when she opened up the image. She'd expected some silly meme poking fun at Edward Logan after their earlier conversation in the Express store. Instead, he'd sent her a dickpic. She couldn't believe it. Her face burned with anger, embarrassment and shame. A heady cocktail of wild emotions coursed through her body and she began to panic, reaching out instinctively for her pills.

Why the hell was James Bygraves sending her obscene images? They'd only just met, as work colleagues. What was he thinking of? He was her age, not a kid. Maybe that's how Mackenzie's generation behaved, but there was nothing about James Bygraves that suggested he would do something as crass as that.

Rosie threw the phone onto the sofa cushion, jumped up, took a pill out of its foil and ran herself a glass of water at the kitchen sink. She gulped down the tablet like it was the cure to the plague, then marched into the hallway to make sure that the front door was locked, hooking the safety chain on and checking twice that it was fastened.

After pacing the hallway for a few minutes, Rosie returned to her phone. Had she imagined it? Sometimes, when she was on the stronger drugs, she struggled to tell reality from fantasy, like that voice in her room that time.

There was never any proof that anybody had been in there with her, touching her leg. She assumed she'd imagined it. Was she making this up as well?

She picked up her phone with the nervous reluctance of a woman who might have been receiving some much-feared test results. The image was still there, a single picture. It was his name too; there was no doubt that it been sent via that account. Rosie deleted the image and checked out the profile. There was nothing; no friends, no likes, no other pictures. It was completely blank. Was this Phil and Terry messing around? Surely not. They were politically incorrect, but both were married men with many years of family life racked up between them. Whatever they lacked in good taste, they were not predatory; they would never do something like that.

Rosie wanted to scream, feeling as if she was beginning to spiral again. She'd been settled for several weeks now and had even begun to think there might be a time when she didn't need any medication.

She closed her eyes and breathed deeply, just as Vera had told her to do. Then she closed down Facebook and gave her friend a call. She needed help, and she needed it straight away.

CHAPTER NINE

After only one day back at work, Rosie was on Skype with Vera. She'd hoped to last out longer than that, but the disturbing image on her phone had badly shaken her. She doubted herself so much that she wanted her friend to see the profile via the laptop's webcam and confirm she wasn't seeing things.

'Do you think it is somebody from the office?' Vera asked. 'It seems a strange thing to send a new work colleague. And you said there's no photograph. It looks like a bad joke to me.'

'I just don't know any more,' Rosie replied, fighting back her tears. She could feel herself teetering on the brink, a familiar place. It was unbearable to imagine returning to the hospital. Her father was too old to be caring for a toddler full time. If he died – God forbid – Sam would be taken into care. It was the one fear that drove her on. It was the worst thing that could happen, the final shame: the realisation that she was no longer capable of even caring for a child.

'Are you going to report it to the police?' Vera continued. Her calm and measured voice always helped Rosie, like a metronome, marking a steady pace: never too fast, never too slow. It moved Rosie along at a tempo she could cope with. If she could just hang onto Vera's words, she'd get through it.

'Should I?' Rosie asked. She hadn't even considered it. The less she had to do with the police and social care, the better. After all, they'd already been called out to her suicide bid at the flyover, along with an ambulance. If she could avoid getting the police involved, that would probably be for the best.

'I certainly think you should have kept the picture as evidence,' Vera continued. 'If it happened again, at least the police would take you seriously.'

'Is it an offence, though?' Rosie asked. 'I mean, we chatted together. Isn't this what millennials use instead of business cards these days?'

'It is an offence, Rosie, and you shouldn't have to put up with it.'

'I like the man – I *liked* the man,' Rosie said. 'He's the last person I would have expected to do this. What the hell makes a guy think that's okay? When Liam and I first met, we went for a coffee and a chat. Our marriage also managed to survive without him ever sending me a nude picture. Maybe we got it all wrong.'

Vera laughed at that.

'Well, some things have certainly changed, that's for sure. Bill and I didn't even sleep together for two years. In all the years I was with him, he never sent me a picture of himself naked. I'd have just laughed, anyway. Mind you, he ended up leaving me for a younger woman, so he turned out to be just as bad as the rest of them. Most of these young-sters can work through their Tinder matches in the time it took us to get into bed with each other. No wonder we see so many of them so screwed up and ending up at Trinity Heights—'

She stopped dead.

'It's alright, Vera. You don't get admitted to that sort of place four times in two years for nothing. I, of all people, know that.'

'But you're different, Rosie.'

Vera's tone slipped back into doctor-patient mode.

'You had every reason to be there. What happened to you would send any sane person over the edge.'

Rosie wasn't so sure, but she was exhausted and wanted the Skype call to end. She'd had enough. Besides, somebody had joined Vera in the room – Rosie could hear them shuffling about away from the webcam – and she could see that Vera was uncomfortable about them continuing the call without the required level of confidentiality.

Maybe she had a new man in tow. Perhaps she had kids; Rosie had never thought to ask and Vera never mentioned it. These chats were informal between friends. They were nothing to do with Trinity Heights; their conversations were strictly off the record. Rosie liked to think of Vera as her friend, but it was a relationship forged in flames.

They ended the call, and Rosie did her night checks before heading up to bed. Liam used to take care of security. He'd work around the switches so that all electrical appliances were turned off properly. She could still hear his voice: *It wastes electricity and could potentially cause a fire at night.*

Liam was always so precise about things. It was a pity he hadn't been more precise about the level of drink he'd consumed that night. He was barely over the limit, but it was enough to invalidate the insurance, turning him into an offender, rather than a victim. Her old friends shunned her because they were unable to navigate the choppy waters of offering sympathy to her while carrying their loathing of a man who'd been over the legal alcohol limit. It was borderline, even the coroner had said it. But it was enough to turn Liam from a good guy to an arch enemy.

Rosie checked the main doors, pushing down on the handles to make sure they were properly locked. She even wiggled the window locks, just in case. How could a single image shake her so severely? She'd seen pictures of naked men before and would see them again, but this one had shocked her.

One of the benefits of being on her current drug regime was that Rosie was quick to fall asleep. Unfortunately, she also experienced vivid and surreal dreams, and often woke up sweating at unearthly hours of the night. So when she jumped up in bed, at 2.37 am, Rosie wasn't particularly surprised. Her dream was filled with the faces of Phil and Terry laughing, fuelled by pints of beer. They were taking pictures of body parts and sending them to her on their phones, all the time laughing, calling her a basket case and saying she deserved it.

Her skin was wet with sweat. She didn't even bother with nightwear any more. It just ended up in the washing basket the next day, anyway. She had enough washing to deal with from Sam, without adding to the mounds unnecessarily. She'd given up changing the sheets, making them last a week. They'd have been in the machine every day, otherwise.

Rosie was convinced she'd heard a sound. She sat up in bed, her heart pounding, and pulled the sheet up to her shoulders, feeling suddenly vulnerable in her nakedness. There was an old t-shirt beside the bed, one of Liam's that she hadn't been able to send to the charity shop when cleaning out his wardrobe. It had a picture of Robert Smith from The Cure on it. They'd been lucky to get those concert tickets, and it had been a brilliant night. It made a great nightshirt too.

She covered herself and got out of bed, then gently pulled back one of the curtains, as if she had something to be ashamed about if someone caught her looking. The street outside was tranquil, cars lined up, parked neat and tight in front of a row of London terraces built at a time when the most action they'd see was a horse coming up the road, with its owner delivering coal or seeking scrap iron.

Her bedroom door was open so she could hear Sam if he stirred. She didn't want to wake him; he'd never get back to sleep if he was disturbed at that time of night. Slowly, cautiously, Rosie picked up her phone and made her way to the open bedroom door, doing her best not to creak the floorboards and being extra cautious passing Sam's room. His door was slightly ajar, the dim night light still providing its protection against bogeymen and monsters. She tiptoed past as if she might trip a land mine at any moment and all hell would be unleashed.

At the top of the staircase, she saw what had disturbed her; something had been pushed through the letterbox and had thudded onto the ground. Her stomach tensed, and she swallowed hard. Who was dropping off letters this late? Not even menus from takeaways were delivered in the middle of the night.

Rosie made her way down the stairs at some speed, anxious to see what had been delivered. It was a white A4 envelope, the type used in a corporate environment. The light from the street lamp outside allowed her to see it had handwriting on the front.

Her phone vibrated in her hand, but she was now intent

on checking the envelope, needing to know what had shaken her peace in the dead of night. She picked it up and turned it around, searching for clues as to what was inside. Her phone vibrated again, but it could wait – this was more important.

The envelope bore her name, house number and street name. She tore it open, placing her phone on the floor to free up both hands. Inside was a copy of the staff handbook that Edward had given her to read. There was a hand-written compliment slip inside.

I found this on your desk. I thought you might want to make an early start over breakfast. Edward.

The sweat covering her body was cold and clammy now, yet her forehead was burning. What was Edward Logan thinking, posting this through her letterbox so late at night? It was intrusive and threatening, like something a bully might say: *I know where you live.*

Rosie stifled a scream as she looked up and caught a glimpse of Liam walking into the dining room at the end of the long corridor. He was holding Phoebe, as he always was when she saw him. Every time, Phoebe was dead. If she was going to see things, her screwed up brain might at least give her an illusion where her child was alive.

Seeing Liam again meant she was on dangerous ground. Her phone vibrated. She picked it up. There were more messages, four of them from James' account on Facebook. She knew she shouldn't look – not in her current frame of mind – but she ran into the flames anyway.

There were four images. She half expected them to be more nudes, but she was wrong. Instead, three of the photos showed a dead rat laying in a desk drawer. It was her desk drawer. The fourth image had been taken at a distance. It wasn't very clear, but she knew where it had been taken.

Somebody had photographed her sitting on the bench earlier that day, eating her baked potato. Haylee was with her.

Rosie didn't care about waking Sam any more. She couldn't even think about his needs. The walls of the hallway closed in on her, dark thoughts crushing her. She screamed loudly and thumped the wall in frustration. As Sam stirred upstairs, she collapsed onto the floor and shuffled into the corner, in a desperate bid to conceal herself. She stayed there until morning, when she was woken by her father's knock at the door.

CHAPTER TEN

Rosie had one more day to get through before the weekend. If she could just make it until Friday evening, she'd get some headspace.

She pretended that everything was fine when her father arrived. By the time his knock at the door had woken her up, Liam's old t-shirt was stuck to her skin where the sweat from the previous night had dried. She'd crawled along the hallway, run up the stairs quietly to grab her dressing gown, given her hair a quick brush through with her fingers, then answered the door as if nothing had happened.

'Morning Rosie, not showered and dressed yet?' her father smiled. He knew better than to judge. She'd noticed some time ago how he seemed to have picked up on what Vera did. He would only prod her gently to do the next thing that needed to be done.

As he stood on the doorstep, Rosie heard the door in the house next to hers opening up.

'Everything OK over there?' came the sound of her neighbour's voice.

Rosie stayed inside her house, unwilling to engage.

'Yes, everything's fine,' Rosie's dad answered. 'Why do you ask?' he added.

'That child was crying for over an hour last night. I almost called the police again.'

Rosie wanted to run outside and tell her neighbour to get stuffed, but she knew she'd have to play it cool. This was just the sort of thing that could get Sam taken away from her. She stepped outside so she could see her neighbour, Anne.

The air was cold and damp, her breath visibly making clouds as she spoke.

'I had a devil of a job nursing him back to sleep,' she lied. 'He was ill last night, and nothing would settle him.'

She felt her father tensing; he knew.

'So long as that's all it was,' Anne replied. 'I was concerned, that's all. What with last time...'

'Thanks so much for checking, we appreciate it,' Iain said, putting a lid on the conversation. 'Come into the house, Rosie. You'll catch your death out here.'

Iain Campbell knew well enough not to force the issue. Rosie saw how her father always scanned the house when he came in, saying nothing, but obviously looking for the signs that things were slipping away from her again.

'Your phone is on the floor here,' he said, bending down to pick it up. He grimaced as he did so. It was his back, nature's curse for so many years of manual labour.

'It's okay dad, I've got it,' Rosie said, picking up her phone and retrieving the envelope and handbook that were still on the floor from the night before.

'Post so early in the morning?' Iain asked.

'Just a bit of light reading from work.'

Rosie tried to brush it off, but she could tell he knew. He was there when she was born, modern like that even back then. Right from the start, he'd been an involved father– he knew his daughter, and could tell she was covering up. He didn't push it, though and Rosie loved him even more for that.

Getting ready for work that morning was a blur of rushing and panic. She showered and dressed at speed, leaving Iain to do the honours with Sam, and skipped breakfast, rushing for the tube and getting there in the nick of time. She needed to slink into the office without seeing James, to give herself time to think things through.

Haylee was at the reception desk when she walked in, ever the company sentinel, watching the comings and goings and exchanging pleasantries with all who passed.

'Is Edward in?' Rosie asked, not even bothering with a greeting.

'Good morning to you too!' Haylee smiled. 'You look like you've been binge-watching Netflix all night. You've got rings around the rings around your eyes.'

'Something like that,' Rosie replied, her mind elsewhere. 'So, is he?'

'When isn't Edward in the office?' Haylee muttered. 'If it wasn't for him signing in and out, I'd swear he spent the night in that office. No doubt hanging upside down from the ceiling, dressed in a black cape.'

She laughed at her own joke and Rosie squeezed out a smile.

'See you later,' she said, rushing off down the corridor. She'd been away two years – almost to the day – yet when she stepped inside that office, it was as if that time had never passed. It was like riding a bicycle. If she thought about it too much, she didn't think she could do it, but when she stepped through the doors, her feet began pedalling and she stayed upright, moving on ahead.

The sound of a raised voice echoed along the corridor. It was Neil Jennings again. This time he wasn't rowing with David. Edward Logan was his latest target.

Rosie had been all fired up to storm into Edward's office and confront him over his midnight visit. But Neil Jennings had taken the wind out of her sails, already with Edward, giving him a piece of his mind. Rosie wondered how long Neil's blood pressure would be able to take it. She knew he could be ferocious at times, but he appeared to be particularly stressed out nowadays.

As Rosie opened up her office door, she saw Mackenzie skulking out of the meeting room opposite. She decided to try again with the new apprentice. They'd got off to a particularly uncomfortable start the previous day.

'Hi Mackenzie, how are things?'

'You know,' Mackenzie answered. 'Another day, another meeting room, more teas and coffees. I'm not sure I'm cut out for the world of work.'

You and me both, Rosie thought.

'It gets easier,' she smiled. 'Before you know it, you'll be retiring with a gold watch.'

'What?' Mackenzie answered gracelessly.

She probably didn't even know what a watch was. Come to think of it, Mackenzie was unlikely to know what retirement was. Her generation would probably never experience it.

'Have a great day,' Rosie said, deciding not to get herself in any deeper. She felt a moment of panic as she stepped into her office. Would she be as useless conversing with her own child when he got older?

She dropped off her lunch in the kitchen, wedging it into the fridge which was packed with half-finished margarine tubs, purchases which hadn't been claimed by the owners for weeks and several items which were no longer identifiable. Various members of staff – some familiar, others not – passed her in the corridor and in the kitchen. She was relieved that there was no sign of James.

The sun was streaming into her office as she stepped inside, and she was immediately grateful for the crass duo of Terry and Phil who had released her from a working life of darkness and isolation. The view over London was stunning. It sent fire through her veins as she surveyed the city from thirteen floors up.

David's head appeared around the door. That was a David Willis signal for *I'm not staying, this is just brief*. He looked tired and worn. Rosie didn't recall him looking like that before. He used to enjoy his work so much.

'I don't think I mentioned next weekend? It's a team-building event initiated by you-know-who. I'm so sorry – I should have mentioned it earlier. I have too many things on my mind. There's a lot going on behind the scenes and I've been distracted. Edward will pass on the details, I'm sure. I hope it doesn't mess things up for you at home? I'll make it up to you, I promise.'

His head disappeared as quickly as it had arrived. David Willis didn't ever need to apologise to her. He had saved her life by keeping her salary flowing, even if it was at a heavily reduced rate. If David had not bought her that time, her life would have caved in by now. He was an angel.

'Good morning!'

It was Edward Logan. He seemed none the worse for his altercation with Neil.

Rosie felt the fury firing up in her the moment she set her eyes on his face. Her hand darted towards her bag, and she pulled out the envelope that had been pushed through her letterbox.

'What on earth were you thinking, posting this at that time of night?'

She tried to keep her voice calm and regulated, but deep down she didn't particularly care about being professional, rational or measured. She just wanted to spit the words out at him like a machine gun, leaving him bloodied and reeling.

Rosie waved the white envelope in front of his face, pointing to the handwriting in extreme frustration as if trying to teach him a lesson which just wasn't sinking in.

'Where does it mention that in your bloody handbook, eh? Where does it say you can wake me up in the middle of the night with something that could have easily waited until morning? I don't care who you are, Edward. You can be the king of all human resources land as far as I'm concerned, but this is just not on – it's not normal. I've worked here for years; it wasn't necessary before, and it isn't necessary now.'

Rosie knew she was out of line, but she had to find a release for the anger she felt at receiving those images on her phone. She was pissed about the handbook, of course, she was. But it was James she was most furious at. She threw the envelope at Edward, and it floated past him and fell onto the ground, the most ineffectual weapon of all time. Rosie stood there, fire in her eyes, challenging him for a response.

Edward Logan was calm. He bent down, picked up the envelope and studied the handwriting on the front. Then, calmly, he gave her his answer.

'That's not my handwriting, Rosie.'

CHAPTER ELEVEN

Not for the first time since she'd returned to work, Rosie would have been happy for the ground to swallow her up and devour her. She hadn't even considered the possibility that Edward might not have delivered the handbook. Every member of staff had one, after all. She'd just jumped to what seemed the obvious conclusion when she saw his name on the compliments slip.

Both Haylee and James had warned her about the new HR man. Maybe she'd been braced for it so much, she had failed to give him the benefit of the doubt.

Rosie looked at him, her mouth wide open, unable to find any words. Her cheeks were growing hot, and Edward wasn't helping matters by standing there, confident and calm, saying nothing.

'I don't know what to say... I'm so sorry,' was the best that she could muster.

'You've been ill. It's only to be expected,' Edward replied.

If that was intended to be comforting, it was anything

but. She was digging her way out of a deep, black hole and it would be impossible to claw her way out if everything she did or said was related back to her mental illness. Even if she knew it was true.

'I want to ask you something, Rosie. Please be honest with me.'

Edward appeared to be changing the subject. His tone was conciliatory, as if he was seeking something from her. Perhaps it was the best thing to do, given the circumstances. It gave them a way out.

'What is it, Edward? I'll help if I can. Especially after accusing you of something you didn't do.'

'What are they all doing when they leave on a Friday?' he asked.

That came out of the blue. Had he caught the scent of the after-work Friday drinks club? It was a good job her face was already red from the embarrassment of her false accusation; she could feel her face burning once again.

'Oh, um, I don't know, Edward. I... er, I haven't been back long enough to know anything. I'm sorry, I can't help. Why, what's going on?'

'They all sneak off on a Friday evening. They think I don't know, but I do. What are they doing that can't include me?'

Rosie studied his face, but it was devoid of any emotion. She didn't know whether to feel sorry for him or to agree with her workmates that he deserved to be excluded from their social gathering. She was saved by the bell.

'That's my phone ringing,' Edward said. 'I'll catch up with you later.'

Edward left the room, and Rosie moved back to the window, admiring the view once again. The phone on her desk rang. She picked it up, not expecting to receive any calls so early in the day.

'Hey, it's just me,' came Haylee's voice. 'I take it you're on for drinks this evening? I came by your office just now, but Edward Sausagehands was with you.'

Rosie laughed. That's what she missed about work, the nonsense and gossip. She didn't get that from Sam.

'Why do you call him that?' she asked.

'Look at his hands next time you see them. He's thin as a rake, but he has puffy hands. It's weird. You'll see.'

'I hadn't noticed, but I'll look more closely next time. Yes, I'm on for drinks. But warn the others, Edward suspects. He was asking me about it.'

'Are you on for lunch again today?' Haylee asked.

'I've got a cheap sandwich that I bought at the Express store last night, but I'm happy to eat it with you in the square – if it's not raining.'

'Gotta go!' Haylee said, and the line went dead. Rosie knew this of old. As a receptionist, the phone could go at any time. Haylee was always on a moment's notice, a slave to the ring tone.

Rosie sat at her desk, removed the handbook from her bag and opened it up where she'd left it the day before. After the weekend, she'd have to dive back into her job properly. She'd need to arrange briefings with the sales team and Neil Jennings at some point, to get up to speed with the new online system and become fully embroiled. She hoped she could remember it all. The professional aspect of her life seemed a million miles away.

Rosie was grateful to get through the morning without further interruption. She'd had a brief encounter with Annabelle Reece-Norton who'd darted her head around the open door to exchange a word or two.

'Morning, Rosie! I thought you were a ghost. It's going to take some getting used to you being in here now. Damn, gotta rush! Edward is on the prowl. I don't want any fifteen-minute time-outs; I'm looking forward to after-work drinkies.'

Rosie heard her accounting for her time further along the corridor as she ran into Edward.

'Just making sure Rosie is up to speed on the new systems,' she said in her cheery voice. Whatever Edward's response was, it stifled her energy, strangled it and left it gasping on the floor for breath. Annabelle's voice was heard no more.

As Rosie worked her way through the staff manual, she glanced over the headlines, mixing occasional reading with thoughts about the late postal delivery and the pictures from James. Had he set up the rat all along? Maybe he'd taken those pictures before removing the dead creature from her drawer, and it was some kind of misguided joke. But what about the nude picture? That was inappropriate, however she looked at it.

Edward's revised handbook didn't cover dickpics. It just offered a few non-committal words about sexual harassment in the workplace (don't do it) and gender-inappropriate humour (don't do it). She reckoned that last page must have been missing in Phil and Terry's copies. Edward's response to everything seemed to be *don't do it*.

Want to pull a sickie after a night out on the booze? *Don't do it*. Need to leave work early because it's your kid's sports day? *Don't do it*. Want to post on Twitter sharing your poignant views on the political hot potato of the moment? *Don't do it*. It left Rosie wondering if there was anything she could still do, now that David's once happy company had passed over to new ownership.

She did her best to avoid James all day and only had one near miss when she went to the kitchen to pick up her sandwich at lunchtime. He was just leaving the kitchen and looked as if he might want to talk to her, so she swiftly changed direction and pretended she was heading for Edward's office. She waited until the coast was clear, then returned to the kitchen, only to find her sandwich had been eaten.

'For Christ's sake!' she cursed as Neil walked in.

'What is it? Fridge wars again?' he asked.

'Some bugger's eaten my sandwich. And they've left half of it in the plastic wrapping like they intend to come back and finish it. Cheeky bugger!'

'You gotta lock stuff down in this place,' Neil advised. 'So many temps now, we hardly know who's working here any more.'

After begrudgingly eating her second baked potato of the week from the snack van, and fighting off the temptation to tell Haylee all about James' impolite photo habit, Rosie made it through the afternoon, putting everything in place to gently increase her tempo and do some real work when she came back into the office the following Monday morning. Before she knew it, it was Friday drinks time.

Edward was on the prowl. It made Rosie want to laugh. He knew something was up, but he couldn't put his finger on it. As much as it was hilarious, there was also something very sad about it. He was so deeply unpopular, yet he couldn't figure out why they didn't want to include him in whatever it was going on.

'Have a good weekend, Edward!' Annabelle called along the corridor.

'What are you up to tonight?' Edward asked.

'Oh, nothing, just TV and a takeaway,' she replied, evasive and non-committal.

'Are you off too, James?' came Edward's voice. He was like a patrol guard, but he couldn't stop the prisoners escaping.

Rosie hadn't thought about James being at the bar. It might be difficult to avoid him. But she couldn't stay long; she had to get back for Sam.

'Yes, have a great weekend, Edward. Anything you need to tell me before I go? I wouldn't want to put you through the trouble of having to come to my house to update me on anything.'

It was Rosie's turn to make her exit. They couldn't all leave at precisely the same time; Edward would soon catch the whiff of betrayal and deceit.

'You're going too?' Edward asked. 'Anybody would think there was a party going on and I wasn't invited.'

'Ha – no, nothing like that,' Rosie replied. 'You know how it is, a busy weekend with lots to do.'

'Yes, and you've got a party on for Sam this weekend – that'll keep you busy.'

Had she told him about that? How did he know?

'Yes, have a nice weekend, Edward. See you on Monday.'

She hadn't seen him like this before. Where the previous evening he'd been all about working hours and doing your duty for the company, now he was anxious; he knew something was going on, but he couldn't quite grasp it.

He'd made no effort to put Rosie at ease since her return, so she was happy to head out of the office without a backward glance. A man like Edward Logan deserved to be left out.

Terry, Annabelle, Phil, Haylee and David were all there, laughing loudly at a table crammed with beers and lagers. James was there too, along with a couple of other people she didn't know yet. She avoided his glance, unable to face that particular conversation.

Terry was in the middle of recounting the story of December's Secret Santa, when he'd replaced the Action Figure toy that had been bought for Edward with a strap-on dildo. As he'd pulled it out of its seasonal wrapping paper, at least ten smartphones had been primed to take a photograph. Every time Edward pissed them off, they'd email each other an image of him holding up the strap-on, a look of discomfort and bemusement on his face, with a suitable retaliatory caption like *Dick head!* or *What a cock!* After so much time away from an office environment, Rosie forgot how much solace could sometimes be found in such petty acts of vengeance.

This wasn't the only thing Rosie had forgotten in the past two years. Even though she'd sworn to keep a close eye on the time, after five minutes she remembered what a great laugh after-work drinks could be. Terry and Phil ought to have used up all of their comedic material by now, but still, it came, joke after joke, well-told story after well-told story. She was laughing so much she almost peed herself.

'Got to go to the toilet!' she said to Haylee, who had tears streaming down her face. 'You'll find out about the perils of pelvic floor muscles one of these days!'

She slid off to the toilets at the back of the pub and texted Iain while she was sitting in the cubicle.

Okay to stay a little later? I'll bring back takeaway.

She was relieved when the reply came in immediately afterwards.

We're fine here, Rosie. Enjoy yourself. You deserve it x

Rosie finished off, washed her hands and double-checked in the bathroom mirror that her skirt wasn't tucked into her knickers. All good, she headed out and ran straight into James. He'd been waiting for her, that much was obvious.

Rosie glanced to the side, sensing that the atmosphere had changed in the bar.

'You've been avoiding me, Rosie. I thought we were pals. What's up, did I do something wrong?'

Why were Terry and Phil so quiet? They'd been laughing their heads off when she left the room.

'You know why I'm avoiding you.'

Why did he even need to ask? A surge of rage sent her heartbeat racing.

'Really, I don't,' James protested. 'What's up, Rosie? Have I offended you in some way?'

'Those pictures you sent on Facebook? What on earth were you thinking sending me dickpics?'

'What pictures? Rosie, what are you on about? I haven't sent you anything – I don't know about any pictures. And I'm far too old-fashioned to be sending you nudes. Besides, I'd lose my job if I did something as stupid as that.'

'It was on Facebook. It came from your account.'

'Rosie, I don't even use Facebook – I hate social media. It's all I could do to join WhatsApp, so I can tag along to these drinking sessions.'

She looked directly into his face, searching for signs of a lie, but she found none.

'Look, let's talk about this,' James continued. 'Whatever you think I've done, I swear, I'm innocent.' He paused and glanced towards the bar area. 'Have you noticed it's all gone quiet out there?'

'Yes.' Rosie nodded. 'Do you think everything's alright?'

She followed James as he moved towards the bar area. They were right. It had gone quiet. The entire group – Terry and Phil included – were sitting in silence with guilty looks on their faces. And standing next to their cluster of tables was Edward Logan, looking like he'd just caught a big mouse in a trap.

CHAPTER TWELVE

It wasn't the most elaborate birthday party for a two-year-old, but it was the best Rosie could do. There had been no parent and toddler groups for her, no succession of children's parties at fancy venues and no play dates in the park. Her friend, Leone, had suffered from postpartum depression, which was how they'd met at Trinity Heights. Leone was a day patient rather than an inmate – as Rosie liked to refer to herself – and they'd hit it off from day one when they met at the snacks machine.

Leone had wanted to smother Owen once upon a time. Rosie had never considered killing Sam, but she did, for a short time, detest and despise his presence. What a glowing couple of new mothers they made. Thanks to a cocktail of modern drugs and the support of people like Vera, they'd navigated the dark tunnels of their minds and emerged into the bright light at the other end.

As Rosie watched Sam and Owen snatching toy cars from each other on the play rug, she consoled herself that the children wouldn't remember much of it. She couldn't recollect any of her own childhood birthday parties until the age of five or six years old. Sam would never know what a crappy day it really was.

'So, how are you doing?' Leone asked, taking a sip of wine. They'd promised themselves one small glass. That couldn't mess with the drugs, surely?

'I managed two whole days at work,' Rosie replied. 'I can't say my heart is in it. Only another thirty-five years to go until retirement. Not long left now.'

Leone laughed.

'I know that feeling,' she replied. 'Oh, I forgot to tell you. I got the all-clear, I'm just getting the light touch from social care now. It's official; I'm no longer loopy.'

Rosie reached out and hugged her friend. In the world of mental illness, no longer being considered loopy was every bit as good as receiving a line of As in your school exam results, or the all-clear in a cancer test. It meant you could move on to the next stage of your life.

'You're still on the meds, though, right?'

Rosie wanted the reassurance of her friend not quite being out the woods yet, as a touchstone to measure her own progress.

'I'm on the lighter stuff now,' she replied. 'You should see the list of contra-indications. I think I'd rather live with depression. Lack of bladder control is one of them. At least that's not a problem – giving birth to Owen already screwed that up!'

They laughed out loud. Rosie had almost forgotten how good it was to chuckle freely. It washed through her in a way the drugs could never do; it renewed her, blasting away the dark thoughts that lingered in shadowy corners. Serotonin was the reason, Vera had explained. The more she got, the better she'd feel, apparently.

Rosie's mind wandered back to the horrors of Friday

night. There was a lot of serotonin flowing that night until Edward Logan turned up, the grim reaper whose presence left laughter and good company as corpses at the roadside. She and James had done the only thing possible when they'd seen him from across the room: they'd hidden in the public bar at the other side of the pub. If he'd caught them having sex in the broom cupboard at work, it might have been slightly less embarrassing.

Like the treacherous colleagues they were, they hid there until the group dispersed ten minutes later, exchanging a few polite pleasantries with Edward then, one by one, making their excuses to escape. Ten minutes – that was all it took for Edward's icy fog to descend and freeze them all out. They watched it from afar, each painful moment playing out in slow motion.

They'd had a lovely time in the other bar. He'd shown her his phone, demonstrated that there was no Facebook on it – or any other social media come to that – and, for good measure, allowed her to flick through his most recent images. There was nothing of interest there. No nude pictures, no dead rats and no pictures of Mackenzie. She would never claim to possess the credentials of a TV cop, but as far as Rosie could tell, James was innocent. It made her wonder who'd stitched him up.

'Do you think Edward noticed our coats on the back of those chairs?' Rosie asked, once their work party had finally dispersed, and Edward had left the pub.

'I hope not,' James answered. 'With any luck, we got away with it. I don't think our work colleagues will be very pleased with us on Monday morning, through. I expect to hear the words *traitor*, *betrayal* and *Judas Iscariot* but anything they say to me will be considerably less torturous than having to explain to Edward why he was excluded from after-work drinks.'

'Penny for your thoughts?' said Leone.

Rosie had been a million miles away. Friday evening already seemed a lifetime ago. Since then, she'd done the graveyard visit. It was now officially two years. Two years since she'd lost her husband and daughter. How could it possibly have taken her so long to gain so little ground?

Rosie thought back to her physical injuries. She almost discounted those, but she'd been confined to a wheelchair in the first months, and there'd even been some suggestion she might never walk again. She never credited herself for overcoming the physical part of her injuries.

When she was all smashed up and covered in medical dressings, there was no problem drawing the sick pay from work. It was the psychological element of her recovery that the new company had problems with. Where there were no cuts, bruises or lacerations, it appeared that the corporate world couldn't care less. She excluded David Willis from that; he understood what she was going through.

'I've met a guy...' Rosie began.

She'd barely begun to articulate it herself, but she and Leone had spoken about terrible, morbid things at Trinity Heights; how long it would take to suffocate if you messed up hanging yourself, if it was really so bad if the social workers found a foster parent for your child, and how to conceal your mental illness from a future employer. While other mothers compared nappy brands and shoe sizes, Leone and Rosie veered to the dark side, sharing thoughts that they dare not even mention to their doctors.

'You're kidding!' Leone smiled. 'Good for you. Is it casual or serious?'

'Just friends at the moment. It didn't get off to the best of starts, but he's nice, and handsome. And laying flowers on Liam's grave yesterday, I thought to myself that it's a respectable amount of time to move on now. If I'm going to recover properly, I have to stop dwelling in the past. Vera told me that.'

'Have you – you know – done anything yet?'

Rosie laughed at that.

'Chance would be a fine thing! He hasn't even been to the house yet. It's only day two of our relationship – on day one I thought he'd sent me a nude picture and was some kind of pervert.'

'A woman has needs, you know,' Leone said.

There was a knock at the door which Rosie only just heard.

'Tell me about it,' Rosie said. 'I'm not sure I'm ready for all of that just yet, but he seems like a nice guy. It's long enough after the accident now. I won't rush into anything, but he's interested, I can tell that much. Maybe a few drinks out, if my dad will babysit. Come to think of it, there's a girl at work who offered to help with that. She's a little unusual, but she seems okay.'

The knocking became louder.

'Would you do me a favour and get that door?' Rosie asked. 'I'll watch the kids and pour a little more wine while your back is turned. I just need to get the sausage rolls out of the oven.'

Leone nodded. 'It would be nice if a few extra drops splashed into my glass while I wasn't looking,' she said, moving towards the doorway.

Rosie picked up the oven glove, opened the oven door and removed the sausage rolls. She was only partially aware of what was going on at the door. Leone wasn't speaking to anybody, but something seemed to be commanding her attention. She thought nothing of it until Leone returned to the kitchen, hiding something behind her back.

'Who was it?' Rosie asked, picking errant flakes of pastry to nibble from the baking tray, whilst trying not to burn her fingertips.

'Oh nothing,' Leone replied, a look of guilt wallpapered across her face. 'Just kids playing knock-and-run, I think.'

She edged towards the kitchen bin.

'Whoa!' said Rosie. 'You're hiding something from me.'

'It's nothing,' Leone reassured her. 'Just forget it.'

A strange feeling had returned to Rosie's stomach, and it had nothing to do with wanting to eat the sausage rolls.

'Show me what's in your hand,' she said.

'Don't say I didn't warn you,' Leone replied. She held up the item.

'It was left unwrapped on the doorstep along with a gift tag. It says *Happy Birthday Sam* on it, no name.'

Rosie looked at the present that had been left for her son.

It was a Chucky doll holding a plastic kitchen knife. There were bloody plastic scars across its face, and its eyes were raging and demented, every bit as terrifying as the doll in the films.

CHAPTER THIRTEEN

By the time Sam was tucked up in bed, and the washing up had been wiped up and put away, Rosie had consumed slightly more wine and far fewer sausage rolls than she'd intended. The arrival of the sinister doll had broken up the party spirit. Chucky dolls tended to have that effect on children's parties.

Leone was doing her best to steady Rosie's nerves, but what could she possibly say that would put her mind at rest? Of all people, she knew the risks of her spiralling and turning the event into something more dangerous than it was.

'You told me what a pair of jokers those two guys are at work. Maybe it was just a prank?' she volunteered.

'That was no joke!' Rosie sobbed, trying to stifle her voice as much as possible so as not to attract the children's attention. 'Besides, Terry and Phil have kids of their own. They may be a couple of fools, but they wouldn't do that.'

'What about this new fellow of yours – James? Is he familiar around kids? Some blokes are so useless they'd mistake a doll like that as an Action Man.'

'Come on, Leone. I know you're just trying to help, but you'd have to be some stupid, feckless idiot to think that would be a suitable gift for a two-year-old. Somebody sent that to me. Probably the same person who's been sending those images. And that late-night envelope. It's someone who knows where I live.'

'Do you think you should tell the police?'

'You know I've had my fill of them. I thought you were supposed to be my friend?' Rosie retorted. Leone knew it had been a simple mistake on Liam's part, not realising the insurance company hadn't automatically renewed the policy. If he hadn't died, he might have been arrested for not having motor insurance.

Only Rosie knew that it had been her job to check; that was one truth she couldn't face sharing with anybody just yet, not even Vera or Leone. It was the guilt she still carried, but which she'd allowed her dead husband to take the blame for.

Things had been tense by the time Leone left the house, and she'd taken a taxi home in the end.

'Can I leave my car outside yours tonight and pick it up first thing tomorrow?' Leone asked. 'Best not to drive; I've had a little too much wine. I'll leave you the keys just in case it needs to be moved, and I'll bring the spare in the morning so you won't be disturbed. Then I'll pick up the key next time I see you.'

'No problem,' Rosie replied, 'Pull it up on the driveway behind my old car. It hasn't been driven in two years; you won't be blocking me in.'

It was sad that the birthday party had taken such an awkward turn after the delivery of the Chucky doll on her doorstep. She needed Leone's friendship and couldn't afford for it to turn sour.

Rosie sat down on the sofa and decided to finish off the bottle of wine. There was just half a glass remaining and it would only turn to vinegar if it didn't get drunk. Her stomach was knotted by the events of that afternoon, but also by the thought of having to return to work the next day. It was more than a week too – there was the away day on the Saturday and Sunday, meaning she'd be working twelve days in a row before she got her next proper break.

As she sat there sipping the final drops of wine, trying to detect if it had any adverse effects on her as a result of being mixed with her medication, she wondered if Edward Logan might consider letting her do some half-day working or perhaps even take some leave, to split up that run of working days. It felt like an eternity.

It was too soon. How could she possibly request leave when she'd been off work for two years at the company's expense? She had broken the sick pay rules too; she'd already taken far too much time off.

Her thoughts turned to the doll, and the letter that had been delivered two days earlier. Her next-door neighbour was like a guard dog when it came to her parenting with Sam; the interfering old cow didn't miss a thing. Rosie wondered if she'd caught a glimpse of the person who'd made those deliveries.

She couldn't go to the police yet, not with her previous form with the local constabulary. She wanted to stay off their radar, if they thought she was in trouble again the social workers might be asked to pay a visit. It was better to keep them out of the mix. If she knew who was trying to spook her, she could at least tackle them directly. If it was someone at work, maybe Edward might consider throwing his handbook at them.

Fuelled by the wine, Rosie stood up and walked to the

bottom of the stairs to listen for stirrings from Sam. Hearing that he was quiet and settled, she strode to the front door, pulled off the security chain and turned the handle, the chill evening air quickly overcoming the centrally heated atmosphere in the hallway.

There was a space the length of two small cars in between Rosie's house and the pavement. Leone's car was parked on the driveway, in front of her own abandoned vehicle. At least her dad had thrown a cover over hers to stop it from rusting. She'd never even considered running the vehicle after the accident. It was almost impossible to contemplate driving again, after what happened.

Something was pinned down underneath Leone's windscreen wiper, catching the breeze.

Bloody pizza leaflets.

It was possible to speak with her neighbour across the small wall which separated the gardens of the terraced properties, but for this conversation, Rosie would have to walk around to get to her door. Anne was in – when wasn't she?

'Have you seen anybody coming into my garden?' Rosie asked when she came to the door. 'Or anybody unusual lurking in the street?'

'Who's looking after that child of yours while you're here?' her neighbour asked.

Rosie wanted to punch her in the face. Instead, she told a white lie.

'Don't worry, my dad's in there watching Sam. So, did you see anybody?'

'Why do you ask?' her neighbour said.

Rosie wished the local police were as vigorous in their investigative duties.

'No reason,' Rosie lied again. 'I just missed a parcel

being delivered. I thought you might have seen someone trying to deliver it?'

Their conversation was soon over. They might be neighbours, but there was no love lost between them.

Disappointed, Rosie walked out onto the pavement and darted back into her own garden. Her attention was caught by the paper flapping in Leone's wiper blade. She decided to do her friend a favour and take it inside the house for disposal.

When Rosie saw what it was, she stopped dead. She'd expected to see a printed leaflet offering free delivery any time she fancied a Margherita pizza or calzone. There might even be a double glazing leaflet thrown in for good measure. Instead, she went rigid when she saw what it was. Someone had placed a double-page spread from a pornographic magazine between the wiper blades. It was offensive content too; whoever left it there had been aiming to shock. They had succeeded.

CHAPTER FOURTEEN

The weekend had been so fraught that Rosie was almost relieved to get back to the office in the end. Edward had called an impromptu staff meeting. They were all packed into the conference room, including David Willis. The buzz among Rosie's friends was about Fridaygate, as it had become known.

Rosie and James were branded lucky rather than traitorous. All those who'd been caught with their pants down by Edward Logan agreed that it was possibly the most painful public experience since Janet Jackson's nip-slip at the Super Bowl.

The chatter and gossip ended the moment Edward arrived. He looked sharp and well-groomed, wearing some shiny new shoes which Rosie clocked because the toe cap was a different colour from the rest. Everybody settled, waiting to hear what Edward had to say.

'Thank you for getting here on time, everybody. I trust you all had a nice weekend and I hope that those of you who attended the Friday drinks soirée got home safely.'

He paused a moment, just long enough for those involved to exchange awkward glances across the room.

'I wanted to brief you all on plans for Saturday and Sunday,' he continued. 'But before I do that, I need to make an important announcement on behalf of the Chief Executive—'

He gulped, and the embarrassed glances changed to nervous looks.

'Head office has announced that we're cutting twenty per cent of jobs in this branch.'

There was a collective gasp and some of them began to mutter. Edward held up his hand.

'That means we have ten jobs to lose here. It's due to increased computerisation – your systems have been updated to run more efficiently since the takeover, and that means many posts will become redundant.'

'When I sold the company it was in agreement that all posts would be assured for a period of three years mini-mum,' David said.

'You wee toe-rag,' Neil Jennings shouted. 'You told me you wanted those figures for forecasting – you did'na say you were picking off people to sack.'

'Which jobs are going?' said somebody else from behind her.

Rosie broke out in a sweat. She couldn't afford to lose the job; she had specialist skills and she'd struggle to find something else.

'It's not yet been determined which posts will go. And David, I'll remind you that the financial arrangements of the sale were covered by a non-disclosure agreement.'

'Which I'll happily adhere to, so long as they're honoured.'

Edward ignored that and carried on regardless.

'The purpose of the event at the weekend is to determine a new structure for this branch.'

'Aye, you mean decide who gets a bullet to the head,' Neil Jennings shouted.

There were murmurs of agreement around the room.

'Might I also remind you, Neil, of the details of our own confidential conversation?'

'Aye, I got a verbal warning for insubordination. I'm not embarrassed to let everyone know. The first and only warning I ever had in my long career, and all because I told this man that he's a first-class wanker. You might call it insubordination, but in Glasgow, we call it speaking the truth, you first-class wanker!'

Edward was shaken. Rosie could see that the only way to get Neil Jennings to back off if he had it in for you would be to file a formal complaint. Neil might be on a tight leash, but she knew him of old; he understood how to slip it and bite when he needed to.

'Members of the senior team will be travelling down in a hire car to maximise working time on the journey down. I'll sort that out, Neil, David, Annabelle and Rosie. The rest of you will be expected to make your way down by train, using second-class travel.'

'Aye, and that's going to be a merry dance travelling on a Saturday with the football fans and shoppers,' Neil cursed. It was as if he was angling for an upgrade to a written warning.

As Edward continued, Rosie was suddenly overcome by an overwhelming sense of panic. Everything crowded in on her: the prospect of losing her job, the pressure of the rat, the pornographic images, the horror doll and the final humiliation of having her own child taken away from her. In that room, at that moment, she imagined she was in a deep grave, alive, and they were shovelling dirt over her.

'Sorry, I need to excuse myself,' she blurted out.

'I'd rather you didn't—' Edward began.

She played her ace – the period card. It was embarrassing, but less so than breaking down mid-panic-attack in a room packed with her colleagues.

'It's that time,' she said to Edward, raising her eyebrows.

'It's not time until I say so,' he replied, missing the reference.

Annabelle leaned over and whispered in Edward's ear.

'Oh, yes, I'm sorry. Fine, go ahead, we'll catch up later,' Edward said, clearly uncomfortable.

Rosie made her exit and ran to the female toilets. She locked herself in a cubicle and took long, deep breaths.

Breathe through it, she told herself, remembering how Vera would place a hand on her shoulder and talk her down.

She was spiralling, and she knew she had to stop it. A wave of irrational fear washed over her, not of anything in particular, just everything at once, imagining all the terrible things that might happen.

Rationalise and distract, Vera would say.

Rosie gently pinched the skin on her own arm.

I'm alright now, she whispered to herself.

I'll be alright in five minutes' time.

I'll be alright today.

I'm safe now.

I don't have to worry at this very moment.

It was working. She felt herself steadying. She closed her eyes, thinking back to a holiday she and Liam had taken the first year they were married. New York – beautiful sunshine – a fantastic experience.

The door to the toilets opened. Maybe somebody else had bolted early; perhaps the meeting had ended.

The footsteps were slow and measured, as if someone was on the prowl. They pushed open the door to the first cubicle. It opened slowly, creaking.

Rosie tensed. What the hell was this?

The footsteps moved to the next cubicle to hers. Again, the door was pushed open. It creaked as it swung on its hinges.

She felt the panic beginning to rise once again.

The footsteps moved in her direction, stopping directly outside her cubicle door. She could see the shoes now: shiny new leather with a different-coloured toe cap. Edward Logan was in the women's toilets, and he had come looking for her.

CHAPTER FIFTEEN

'Should you be in here, Edward?'

Thank God, it was Annabelle's voice, come to save her. Rosie sat on the toilet seat, her whole body rigid, hardly daring to breathe. She considered speaking for a moment and feigning mock outrage. That might place Edward on the back foot. But Annabelle was doing an excellent job of making him squirm, so she opted for stealth.

'One of the things we're assessing for the future is unisex toilets; I did check that nobody was in here first.'

Lying bastard! Rosie thought, almost blurting it out loud.

'Well, I'd like to use the facilities, Edward, and as they're not unisex yet, I'd appreciate it if you gave me a bit of privacy.'

'Yes, er... of course.'

'Maybe you could send a memo around letting everybody know about the proposals for unisex toilets. A heads-up might save the other members of female staff getting the kind of shock I just did.'

Good old Annabelle – always polite, but firm. Rosie

wanted to burst out of her cubicle and give her a hug. She listened as Edward made his quiet exit from the female toilets.

'Rosie? Are you still here?'

Rosie slid the lock and pulled the cubicle door open.

'I thought you must be in there. What a creep that man is. The moment the meeting ended, he headed straight here. I knew what he was up to. He wanted to find out if you were putting it on with the period line.'

'I was,' Rosie confessed. 'But I had to get out of there.'

She stood up and stepped out of the cubicle, noticing some graffiti which had been scrawled just below the toilet roll holder.

Please wipe thoroughly to remove all evidence of Edward Logan

'Nice to see Edward has inspired some toilet cubicle art,' Rosie smiled. 'It's quality vandalism too – the spelling and punctuation are correct.'

Annabelle laughed.

'I've never known a man divide a workplace so effectively. He's like an angel of death – particularly now these job losses have been announced. Is that why you excused yourself?'

For a woman whose life was all about numbers, Annabelle Reece-Norton had an uncanny ability to interpret human emotions. Maybe she had a formula tucked away on a spreadsheet somewhere. Either way, she'd managed to hit the nail directly on the head as far as Rosie was concerned. She felt her eyes begin to well up, the very thing she'd been trying to avoid when she left the conference room.

'Oh, Annabelle, I feel like everything is such a mess. I really need this job, even though I'm not even sure I'm still capable of doing it. It's been so long since I did anything that didn't involve cleaning the crap off Sam's arse or trying to keep my sanity intact.'

Annabelle gently placed her hands on Rosie's arms and pulled her towards her, giving her a hug. At that moment, it was precisely what Rosie needed. Annabelle was silent as the two of them stood there, Rosie now sobbing quietly.

'My life is such a mess,' Rosie continued. 'I daren't tell anybody, for fear that they'll commit me to Trinity Heights, take Sam away from me or fire me from this job. We're all supposed to be getting touchy-feely about mental health, aren't we? It seems that admitting you're struggling with psychological issues is the best way to volunteer for redundancy.'

'Hello? Is anybody there?'

Rosie looked up, trying to figure out who Annabelle had called out to.

'It's okay,' Annabelle said. 'Probably someone was coming in for a pee and thought better of it when they heard us talking. I just heard the door open, then close, that's all. Are you still feeling that bad?'

'Yes,' Rosie said, looking directly into Annabelle's face. 'Some things that have happened here are making me wonder if I'm going mad.'

'You and me both,' Annabelle. 'We've both worked here in much saner times. I've been looking for a job on the quiet since the day after Logan arrived. The man is an idiot; who would ever think to put him in charge of a company merger? He has all the empathetic skills of a concrete block. He's in HR too – you'd think a bit of empathy would be a pre-requisite for that job.'

Rosie forced a smile through her tears. She moved away from Annabelle towards a mirror.

'I look a bloody mess,' she said. 'This was the one thing that I promised myself I wouldn't do when I got back to work. How long did I last? No more than three days.'

'Cut yourself some slack, Rosie. You've been through a lot of shit in your life; you can't just roll up back at work and think it's all over. Work through it at your own pace. And forget Edward Logan – I suspect David may have something up his sleeve.'

Rosie dabbed her eyes with a paper towel, trying not to make them look any redder.

'Really?' she asked, turning away from the mirror. 'Is something going on?'

'Well, you heard how pissed off David was in that meeting. He's been mumbling for some time about Silverline Supply Chains not honouring the details of their contract. I think he might try to get the company back.'

'He'd better move fast. They might destroy it before he can do that,' Rosie replied. 'I should show my face again, otherwise I'll be getting one of these penalties that Edward keeps imposing and I'll have to stay on an extra quarter of an hour after work.'

'Just tell him the machine needs re-stocking with sanitary towels and ask him what he's going to do about it. Any mention of lady-issues and Edward looks like an inept teenager – it works every time.'

'Thanks for looking out for me, Annabelle.' Rosie said. She meant it. She needed friends.

They stepped out of the toilets and headed back to their respective offices. The tension was almost tangible; the news of the impending redundancies seemed to have made even the fabric of the building fraught and nervous.

Rosie's office door was open, as she'd left it. The view over London was the first thing that drew her eye as she entered. It was a mystery why anybody would cover that window, even if it did prevent the paperwork from fading; it was a spectacular sight.

There was something on her desk, the position suggesting it had been thrown there rather than placed. She'd missed the excitement of a brown memo envelope. Who knew what it held in this Russian roulette of corporate nonsense? Would it be an invitation to a strategy meeting, to review the previous plans which were failing to deliver? Would it be some office trivia, like a warning to remove decomposing food from the fridge, or a threat to incinerate all abandoned cups with more than one centimetre of mould growth?

How about that firm favourite of hers, a passive-aggressive gripe about not hiding cutlery in personal drawers because it was for the use of all staff? Memos were an endless source of office entertainment, providing a flow of information and gossip that kept the wheels grinding.

Rosie flicked open the envelope. It wasn't a single page of A4 like she'd expected; there was something different inside. She pulled it out. The paper was more substantial, and something was printed on it.

She turned it over. It was a photograph, taken at some distance, across a busy pub. It showed her and James talking at the public bar in the pub the previous Friday. Rosie's mind began to race. Who'd been there that night? Who could have taken the photo? Was this Edward Logan doing some kind of sinister surveillance?

She walked over to the window, her eyes darting between the photo and the view. Anybody could have taken that picture. It was grainy and poor quality, but obviously showed her and James. They all had mobile phones. It would only take a moment to get a photo like that. Nobody used cameras or flashes any more, so anyone could take a picture of somebody else in a public place, and the subject would be none the wiser.

So who was it? Was it one of her colleagues winding her up about how she and James had sloped off to avoid the awkward situation with Edward?

'Hiya!'

It was Mackenzie Devereux, a pile of files in her hands. Her eye make-up looked even more severe than it had done before. It was like looking at an extreme version of Lisbeth Salander.

'Don't mind me, just filing again.'

'Hi Mackenzie,' said Rosie, shaken out of her distraction. 'You haven't seen anybody in my office today, have you?'

'Nah, we've all been in that meeting. Bit of a bummer, wasn't it? I've never seen so many adults shitting themselves in one place before.'

She seemed amused at her own comment. For a moment, Rosie felt a surge of anger towards her. She was probably still sponging off her parents and had no concept of how important it was to keep the salary flowing in. One disruption to the family budget and the entire house of cards could come falling down. Then she had a more sympathetic thought; that Mackenzie's generation would probably never be able to afford their own homes. Either way, both generations were screwed.

'What happens to the memos nowadays, Mackenzie? They used to get picked up from our trays and distributed around the building with the morning post. Does that still happen?'

'Don't think so,' Mackenzie replied, delivering her words whilst manipulating a piece of chewing gum in her mouth. Rosie wondered if she was powered by the stuff; she seemed unable to get by without a bit of gum rolling around in her mouth like a sock in a tumble dryer.

There was a loud shout from along the corridor. Both Rosie and Mackenzie stopped in their tracks and looked at each other. For a second, Rosie thought it was Neil getting wound up about something again. But this was more urgent; it was the sound of somebody who'd been hurt.

Rosie moved swiftly to the door. Other staff members had heard it too and were beginning to emerge from their offices to investigate.

'It came from the kitchen,' Rosie said, speeding up along the corridor. She was first there.

David Willis was lying on the floor, motionless, his face grey, his eyes closed.

'David!' said Rosie, rushing up to him.

She was soon joined by her colleagues who'd also heard the cry. There was a collective gasp of shock as they saw what had happened.

'Is he dead?' came Mackenzie's voice from the small gathered group.

'I don't know,' Rosie replied, as she felt for a pulse.

CHAPTER SIXTEEN

'I can't believe David won't be there,' Rosie said, gulping down the last bite of toast. 'It feels like we've lost the heart of the company.'

Her dad had everything in control. Given that she had to work the weekend, things could have been worse. Sam was content, mangling a Marmite soldier, Iain had bought himself a newspaper on the way over and was happily reading the TV pull-out, and Rosie was ready in time. In fact, she had at least another five minutes before Haylee arrived with the hire car.

'How is he now?' Iain asked, looking up from his reading. 'I've known guys of his age have heart attacks, and they never returned to work. In my line of business, they were on the scrap heap after that.'

'It was only a mild attack, what they call a wake-up call, I think. He'll make it through, but we could have used his support over this weekend. I think it might end up becoming a blood bath.'

Rosie had had five days to get used to the idea of redundancy. Although terrified at the prospect, she'd begun to formulate plans. She'd uninstalled the Facebook app from her phone and used the time she'd have spent on it to register with agencies and job search sites instead. Fortunately, there seemed to be a lot of new ways to go job-hunting since she'd landed her job at David's firm.

She'd refreshed her CV, glossing over her sustained absence. Because she'd been continuously employed, with no gap in employment in terms of her receiving salary, she could get away without mentioning her recovery period. It was more of an omission than a lie; a little like the sleight of hand about who'd been responsible for renewing the car insurance.

'He's lucky he works in an office,' Iain said. 'At least he can still make a living shuffling paper, or whatever it is you corporate people do all day.'

Iain Campbell had never understood how Rosie made a living. If it didn't involve shovels, lorries, sand or cement, it was all a mystery to him.

'They'll be here soon.' Rosie said, 'I'll clean my teeth, then I'm on my way. Thanks for doing this, Dad. I promise it won't be forever. You'll get your retirement soon.'

She placed her hand on his shoulder, and he moved his own up to give it a gentle squeeze. His hands were worn, wrinkled and covered with liver spots. When had he got so old?

As Rosie finished in the bathroom, she heard something drop through the letterbox at the bottom of the stairs.

'I'll get it!' she shouted.

It was the first day she'd been at home late enough to hear the post arriving. She'd been tense all week, expecting more worrying packages or pornographic images. They hadn't arrived, either at home or at work. She wished she hadn't deleted the pictures on her phone.

In her less confident moments, she wondered if she'd imagined it.

No, she'd held the pages of the pornographic magazine in her hands and the Chucky doll was real – Leone had seen that too. She hadn't imagined it. Someone was screwing with her, but they seemed to have lost interest at last. Although she'd been on edge and unsettled for the past five days, nothing new had happened. And if more images had been sent via Facebook, she didn't know. She'd stopped checking it for now.

Rosie came down the stairs.

'That'll be a pile of Valentine's Day cards!' Iain called from the kitchen.

'I doubt it,' Rosie replied. But as she said it, she noticed a pink envelope among the bills. She felt a momentary surge of expectation. Was it from James? They'd been getting on well in an office-only kind of way, chatting in the corridors and co-ordinating tea-breaks in the kitchen. Friday after-work drinks had been put on ice until they could re-group and come up with a new plan to evade Edward Logan.

'There won't be enough of us left with jobs to go for Friday drinks,' Neil Jennings said.

Rosie tore open the pink envelope, not wanting to view it in front of Iain. As the envelope was opened, a cascade of glitter flew out onto the carpet at her feet.

'For God's sake!' she cursed.

'Everything OK?' Iain called.

'It's fine dad. Somebody has sent me a card and the envelope's been filled with glitter. It's made a right mess on the carpet.'

She pulled out the card. The front image wasn't visible because it had been placed face down. She turned it over and gasped. The front was covered with obscene photos which looked like they'd been printed out from the internet. Inside the card it read *Happy Valentine's Day, Rosie x.*

Rosie felt her cheeks burning again and sensed a sick emptiness in her stomach. She had to report this to the police now; she couldn't ignore it any longer. Was it James? He seemed to be the obvious candidate, but she liked him and simply couldn't believe he'd do something so crass.

There was the sound of a car horn outside.

'They're here,' Rosie said, walking through to the kitchen. 'I'm so sorry, Dad. I'll have to leave that glitter mess for you to vacuum – I've got to rush.'

She tucked the card into her coat pocket and placed the unopened bills onto the worktop. Then she kissed Sam on both cheeks – much to his amusement – and gave Iain a quick kiss on his head.

'Have a good weekend,' Iain smiled, 'And don't worry about Sam and me. We've got two days of fun all mapped out.'

'Thanks, Dad.'

Rosie put her coat on and picked up her weekend bag, prepared the night before. Even that simple act proved she was getting a firmer grip on things. She'd turned up at the office for seven days and managed to get on top of the washing and shopping well enough to spend a night away from home. That would have been unimaginable six months previously.

As she stepped out of the front door with glitter on her shoes, she faltered for a moment, trying to spot her colleagues in their car hire on the street. A car horn sounded, and Rosie followed the source of the noise. Tucked into a small gap on the opposite side of the road was a bright red Fiat 500, possibly the smallest car known to mankind that didn't come from the Dinky range.

Are you kidding? she thought.

Packed into the back were James and Neil, looking like over-sized children. Haylee was driving, and Mackenzie was in the passenger seat. It made tube travel look positively spacious. Haylee's window slid down.

'Good morning, Rosie! Look what that fool Edward Logan hired for us.'

'This is a joke, isn't it?' Rosie asked. 'Is there even a seat-belt for me in there?'

'That fuckwit messed up the hire car rental,' Neil cursed. He looked like he was about to explode at any moment.

'They had to substitute with this car,' Haylee said, 'It wasn't entirely his fault. They're short on cars this weekend.'

'Aye, but if he hadn'a been such a skinflint, they'd have substituted it with something bigger,' Neil cussed.

Rosie moved round the back and flicked open the boot. It was already packed with overnight bags.

'Does anybody have anything breakable in their bags?' Rosie asked. 'I'm going to have to ram these down to get them all to fit in.'

With some difficulty, she achieved her objective. It was a good job none of them had over-packed.

Mackenzie got out of her seat and stood on the pavement.

'That's really thoughtful of you Mackenzie,' Rosie said, 'letting me have the passenger seat.'

'I'm not,' she said bluntly. 'I get car sick, so I've got to go in the front.'

'Oh,' was all Rosie could think to say. Yet again, Mackenzie had left her searching for a response. She didn't appear to be malicious in any way, it was just that she seemed oblivious to the responses that other people were giving her.

Rosie climbed into the back of the car, greeting James, who shuffled into the middle seat.

'Hi, Rosie. There are only two seat belts, so I've volunteered to be crash test dummy.'

'That's illegal, isn't it?' Rosie asked.

'Aye,' said Neil, 'but do you want to be the poor bastard who doesn't turn up when we're all fighting for our jobs?'

He made a good point. Rosie forced herself into the small gap that James had left. The seat was warm, at least. Her hips jammed tight against his, giving her a flutter of excitement at the close physical contact.

'All sardines present and correct?' Haylee asked. 'Off we go, for a weekend of bonding and corporate nonsense.'

It was soon very uncomfortable in the car. The windows steamed up fast with five adult bodies on board, and the weak fans in the dashboard struggled to disperse it. They'd foolishly worn their coats because there was no room in the boot for them, adding to the discomfort, and the odour of fresh sweat soon permeated the enclosed space. Their legs were crushed against the seats in front. The only blessing was that it was only just over an hour to their destination.

'I thought Edward was travelling with us?' Rosie asked, as they finally neared the end of their wretched journey and were within spitting distance of their destination. 'Don't get me wrong. I'm not missing being jammed in a car with him. I just thought the senior team were travelling together.'

'Well, with David recovering in hospital, it seems that Edward has made a few changes to the agenda. He wanted Mackenzie to attend, but it was too late in the day for her to join the others on the same train and seat bookings, so she got David's place. Edward decided he was travelling by train with Annabelle, so they could discuss some numbers on the way down.'

'Second-class tickets, I hope?' Rosie said.

'Fuck that,' said Neil. 'They're both in First, Annabelle told me. I challenged Edward about it. He said they needed the space and confidentiality of First in order to discuss management issues. Prick!'

'You're looking pale, Neil. Are you okay?' James asked.

'Well, Mackenzie isn't the only one who suffers from travel sickness, but it would be impolite of me to ask a wee girl to sit in the back,' he whispered.

'We're almost there now – here's the conference centre. Hold on tight. They have speed bumps along the driveway.'

Right on cue, the car reared up at the back, then crashed back down, leaving the stomachs of the rear seat passengers somewhere in between.

'Jesus!' said Neil.

'So, did you get any cards for Valentine's Day?' James said to Rosie, a smile on his face like he was teeing her up for a joke. 'After our conversation the other day, I thought you might like to receive one from a friend. You seemed like you might need cheering up.'

Rosie felt a fiery rage rise up.

'For fuck's sake, James, did you send me this abomination of a card?' Her hands moved to her coat pockets. It was so tight in there that she struggled to retrieve it. She held it up to him, right in front of his face.

The car bounced for a second time, shaking violently.

'Sorry everybody, I took that one a bit fast,' Haylee admitted.

James examined the card.

'Damn it, Rosie, I didn't send you that! Mine had a

picture of some lovely wildflowers on it with a cinema voucher inside it, so you could treat yourself to a night out. You don't think I'd send you something like that, do you?'

'I need to get out,' said Neil.

'Who the hell knows?' Rosie raged. 'For all I know, it was you who sent that dickpic. And put the porno magazine on Leone's car.'

'I don't know what you're talking about, Rosie.'

The car crashed down from a third speed bump, and Neil could hang on no longer. He was sick, and in the confined space there was no avoiding it – the three of them in the back seat were covered in it.

'Damn, I'm pleased I got the front seat,' Mackenzie said. 'That might have been me.'

CHAPTER SEVENTEEN

It wasn't the best of starts to a staff bonding weekend, but at least Neil had succeeded in getting intimately acquainted with James and Rosie. He was horrified.

'I'm so sorry,' he said, 'I thought I could hang on 'til we got to the end of the drive. Dinnae fret, I'll pay for the cleaning. Damn it, I feel like some stupid wee bairn.'

Rosie felt partly to blame. Neil had been asking to get out of the sardine tin, but she'd been so busy accusing James that they'd completely ignored his pleas.

They let Haylee check them all in, out of embarrassment for the condition of their clothing. Rosie, James and Neil slid off into the toilets to clean themselves up as best they could, pending delivery of their room keys. By the time they had all gathered in the reception area once again, Haylee had their bags and their key-cards waiting.

'The rest of the staff have arrived already and are starting to gather in the Inspiration Lounge,' she began.

Neil chuckled at that, his disdain for corporate nonsense undiminished by a bit of travel sickness.

'Here are your room keys. The reception desk has

arranged for a mobile valeting service to take care of the car, so it will smell delightful by the time we have to travel back home in it. If you bring your clothes down in one of these bags, they'll get them express cleaned for you. See? All sorted.'

'That's why you're such a great wee receptionist Haylee,' Neil replied, 'Thanks for that, I appreciate it.'

That was the pussy cat Rosie knew and loved. Neil Jennings was a perfectly decent man, only made unreasonable by idiocy and incompetence.

They took their key-cards, checked their room numbers and headed off in different directions: Neil and Haylee towards the elevators and James, Mackenzie and Rosie towards the door which led to the ground-floor rooms.

'Looks like we're all together,' Mackenzie said. 'You guys stink of sick. I'm going ahead.'

She raced forward, allowing the fire door to swing back in their faces.

'Nice,' James said. 'What a well-mannered young lady.'

'I'm sorry I chewed you out back there,' Rosie said, aware that it might have been a bit heavy for such a confined space. And perhaps not the best timing.

'Look, if you don't believe me, you'll see when my card arrives in the post on Monday morning,' James replied. 'I didn't send you that pornographic one. I wouldn't do something like that. What do you take me for?'

Rosie knew she'd jumped to conclusions. As they worked their way along the long corridor, it quickly became apparent that they'd been placed in adjacent rooms.

'This is embarrassing,' said James. 'If you'd rather I got a new room, I'm happy to go back to reception and change it. I don't want you to feel uncomfortable.'

'It's fine, James, honestly. I believe you. And it was a

nice thought sending me a card. I'll look forward to seeing it when it arrives.'

'Did you keep the weird card?' he asked. 'For evidence. You should speak to the police if you've been receiving stuff like that. It's an offence, and whoever did it can get in some real trouble.'

'I threw it in the bin outside the conference centre,' Rosie replied, slotting in her key-card. 'It was fragranced with *aroma de Neil.*'

James burst out laughing, sliding his own key-card into its slot.

'Right, well let's get cleaned up and make sure we're not late for Edward's presentation - you know how he hates people being late.'

James moved through his door and Rosie followed suit. She was as confident as she could be that James was telling the truth. So who had sent the card? It had to be somebody at work, if the memo on her desk was anything to go by.

She only had ten minutes to peel herself out of her soiled clothes and put them in the cleaning bag that Haylee had given her, then jump in the shower, dress, dry her hair and make sure she looked in a fit state to attend a formal meeting. As she switched off the hair drier, she heard a door opening immediately across from her room, then a familiar voice. It was Mackenzie.

'Yeah, well, whatever,' she said, obviously speaking into her phone. 'Yeah, it's boring as fuck, but at least they have to pay me, 'cause I'm an apprentice and all that.'

Her voice faded as she made her way along the corridor. There was a knock at her door. It was James.

'Ready?' he asked. 'Let's do this. Don't forget your clothes bag.'

As they made their way along the corridor, Rosie

stopped, considering whether to ask James something of a sensitive nature. She decided to go ahead.

'Do you think there's anything unusual about Mackenzie?' she asked.

James stopped walking and laughed.

'I'd say there's a lot that's unusual about Mackenzie,' he said. 'But nothing that a decade or so of work and adult life won't sort out. She's young and graceless, that's all. She'll learn. Why do you ask?'

'Well, she's just so... blunt. And rude. And she knows everything about me – she's been checking me out online.'

'Don't you do that?' James asked.

'Well, yes – but I don't tell them what I found out about them,' Rosie smiled.

'Exactly!' James said. 'We all do. I checked you out, and I bet you tried to check me out too?'

'Yes, I suppose I did.'

'We all do it; it's just that Mackenzie hasn't learned how to be discreet about it yet. It's the internet equivalent of watching your neighbours from behind the net curtains. We just don't admit to doing it.'

'And what did you find out about me?' Rosie asked.

'Nothing that I hadn't heard through the grapevine already. I'm very sad for what happened to you. It doesn't matter who was to blame for what – as far as I can see, your life was wrecked two years ago and so was the life of your child. It was horrible, but it was just a tragic accident. They do happen, you know. Somebody doesn't have to be crucified every time. We're all human and we all make mistakes sometimes.'

They'd handed over their washing bags at reception and were almost at the Inspiration Lounge, though Rosie had little expectation of inspiration playing any part over the next two days. They were five minutes late too. She knew enough about Edward Logan already to know that he would notice.

'You ready?' James asked as they stood outside the double doors of the conference room. 'We'll jump together like we're doing a parachute drop. No chickening out. After the count of three, ready?'

'Thanks for saying what you said,' Rosie whispered, 'About the accident. I appreciate it. Most people go on a witch hunt. I've had very little sympathy about what happened.'

Edward had already started his presentation when they sneaked through the doors and he was in full flow.

'...so, contrary to what I told you in Monday's meeting, we're now going to have to cut the existing staff by 25%.'

He looked up and saw them standing by the entrance, searching for a place to sit.

'Oh, good of you to join us, James and Rosie. I had the conference centre staff take the extra seats away, as I didn't think we'd be needing them. I hope you don't mind standing for this session.'

'Arsehole!' came Neil's barely concealed voice. He was sitting at the back of the room in what might traditionally be regarded as the naughty boy's seat.

Mackenzie looked like she'd made it in the nick of time, having found a place to sit, even though she'd only been a few minutes ahead of them.

'Damn pleased I'm just an apprentice,' she began. 'You lot are screwed. I'm so glad I don't have a mortgage to pay.'

CHAPTER EIGHTEEN

This was Edward's show, and if it were possible to gain superhuman powers from HR deliverables, he was Thor at that moment, holding the room in the palm of his hand as he talked about redundancy procedures, compensation packages, notice periods and re-training support. Then he threw a grenade into the room.

'When you signed your new contracts with Silverline Supply Chains, you varied your terms and conditions for redundancy payments. Those of you with long service will find that your compensation arrangements have been reduced. David Willis offered a very generous package which we were unable to sustain.'

'Aye, but David Willis managed to keep this company profitable for three decades before you expensive-suited tossers came in and screwed it up!'

Neil Jennings' fury filled the room. As one of the longest-serving members of the team, he'd just discovered that he would have to work another ten years to receive the same pay-off that he would have done a year ago. He didn't look like he was going to manage another ten minutes under Edward Logan's stewardship.

Rosie ran the numbers in her head. She'd clocked up a decent period of service, and her redundancy payment might cover a few debts, but she was much too young to be contemplating retirement and that Holy Grail of all workers, a fully funded pension.

'You know what? Fuck this!' Neil Jennings cursed. The room was silent, as it always was when Neil had his say. As far as Rosie could see, in spite of the fact that he looked like he might murder Edward Logan, there was a lot of love for Neil Jennings in that room. He was saying what they were all thinking in exactly the way they'd like to say it. When it came to conveying outrage, anger, contempt and frustration, the Glaswegian accent sounded like it had been invented for such occasions.

'You can stick yer bloody redundancy package where the sun don't shine,' Neil cursed, throwing his paperwork on the floor. 'I'm telling yer this contract change is irregular and illegal. I'll be spending the rest of this weekend reading up on company legislation on company time. And if yer don't like it, yer wee tosser, call me in for another disciplinary on Monday morning. 'Cause it's official, yer wee jobby, Neil Jennings no longer cares!'

He stormed out of the room, and there was a round of applause from his colleagues. Neil Jennings had just articulated their thoughts, feelings and frustrations, though they would never have had the courage to do it.

'Damn, he's good!' said James. 'There's a chair free now – want to share it?'

Rosie nodded, and they moved over to the vacant seat while Edward adjusted his dignity. Despite the scene Neil had just caused, Edward still commanded the room; however much contempt he was held in, he had their futures in his hands.

'This feels comfortable after that car ride,' Rosie whispered. 'I've got more space on this half-chair than I did in that. It's positively luxurious by comparison.'

For a moment – and only for a moment – Rosie caught a glimpse of her former self. She was flirting with James, joking about and enjoying it. Although the occasion was a grim one, she was with her work colleagues and engaged in corporate life. And, if only for a second, that sense of them all being in the same boat, that joy of laughing with a colleague, made her feel like her old self again. It felt like they were all gathered there for the world's worst sermon, but in spite of everything, Rosie saw a future for herself in that conference room, a feeling that had taken two years to rekindle.

Edward had recovered himself. It was evident that whenever Neil Jennings had a go at him, he would assume the appearance of a Windows computer carrying out a re-boot. Fortunately for the attendees, it didn't take long for Edward to execute a re-start. He would be out of things for around half a minute, then he would start talking again. With the applause now over for Neil's outburst, Edward was ready to continue, as if nothing had happened.

'So, here's how we're going to manage this process...'

'He's like that molten metal Terminator,' James said, 'When a bullet's fired through its head, it looks shocked for a couple of seconds, then it carries on trying to rip your head off.'

Rosie burst out laughing at the image. It was entirely out of keeping with the mood in the room.

'Sorry,' she said, as some of the newer staff members glanced impatiently at her.

Rosie felt like a giggling school-girl, admonished by the teacher, but unable to obey the instruction to settle down. She was shaking on the seat as she tried to stifle her laughter, aware of James smiling beside her.

Joy was to Edward Logan what a wasp was to the rest of the world; when it was in the room, it had to be squashed, and the sooner, the better. Edward had just the tool to swat this pest.

'We're going to complete several exercises today which will help us to isolate the posts which will be in scope for redundancy. This first exercise is one I devised myself, to enable us to get a better sense of what holds the company back and what oils the wheels. I call this process *Spanners in the works.*'

'Is he allowed to do this?' Rosie asked. 'I thought there were procedures for making people redundant. This feels like a Wild West version of it.'

'I suspect they know who's going already,' James replied. 'This will just be some half-arsed exercise to make us feel like we have some control over our fate.'

'If you look in your document packs for the accompanying worksheet, I'd like you to take a few minutes in silence to note down behaviours which you feel may inhibit the success of the company.'

Edward looked like he was auditioning for Simon Cowell; never had a man looked so much like this was his big moment.

'I will be doing the same thing, and we'll add our results to the whiteboard.'

The room descended into silence. An attentive member

of the staff from the conference centre had brought in an extra chair, and James took it from her. Rosie felt disappointed that he had moved; the physical contact gave her a thrill which she hadn't experienced for some time. The only close male contact she'd had were the professional hands of the medical staff and the family contact with Sam and Iain. She was ready for something more now, and that felt good. It meant she was emerging from the darkness.

The room remained hushed until Edward called time on the activity. There was a low murmuring as he asked people to stop writing down their ideas, then he picked up a marker pen and poised himself to start writing down responses from the staff.

'There are no right and wrong answers here,' he began. 'You may think that some behaviours should be supported in the workplace. This exercise is all about thinking things through from the company point of view. For instance, here are some behaviours that I would consider very disruptive, to get the ball rolling.'

He began writing on the whiteboard. With every movement he made, the pen squeaked loudly.

'Somebody needs to oil Edward,' Rosie whispered, and she burst out laughing again.

'I'm sorry, Edward,' she said, her face reddening. Sometimes her drugs made her emotions feel more extreme. They were certainly doing it at that moment. She hadn't experienced a sense of naughty fun for a long time, and she was getting carried away with it.

'I think there's a mouse in the room,' James whispered back, as the squeaking continued. The giggling was contagious. Rosie watched as shoulders began to shake at the squeaking sound, but Edward appeared oblivious to its comedy potential. He glared at Rosie.

'From the employer's viewpoint, prolonged illness can be very disruptive to a business,' he began. 'As can maternity leave and bereavement. All of these situations place a long-term burden on a company and can create a lot of pressure around a post.'

Rosie's giggling was stopped dead in its tracks. There was no doubt that he was alluding to her situation, even without mentioning her name. He was threatening her, reminding her that she was a burden on the company.

'I'll add one more, then we'll take your ideas,' Edward continued. 'Insubordination.'

'He's scapegoating Neil now – this is outrageous,' James said.

'Challenging the authority of superiors is time-wasting and counter-productive.'

Rosie expected Neil to chip in with an *Aye, but what if your boss is a wanker?* comment, then remembered he'd left the room.

If she'd experienced some much-missed joy that morning, Rosie was now back in her dark place, worrying about the future, fearing for Sam's security and embarrassed at her weakness after Liam died. Edward had put it in a nutshell; she was a burden. All the time she couldn't get her head straight, she was excess baggage; to her company and her father. And for her son, she was a liability.

'This is like the Hunger Games,' James said quietly.

'More like corporate genocide,' said a woman who was sitting behind them. Rosie didn't know her.

'Fuck this!' came a man's voice. 'Neil Jennings has got this right. I refuse to take part in this process.'

It was a grey-haired man who Rosie knew only vaguely. He was another with long service at the company. Redundancy would deal him a crushing blow at his time of life. He stormed out of the room.

'And there you have it,' Edward said, with a smirk. 'Sometimes, during this process, people self-select. They actually volunteer for redundancy. It looks like we're moving towards our 25% goal already.'

CHAPTER NINETEEN

Edward's exercise was every bit as demoralising as the 'spanners in the works' title suggested, and Rosie was worn out by the time the day came to a close at five o'clock. If there was one good thing about Edward Logan, it was that he always finished on time.

The day had been an uncomfortable mix of veiled threats, depressing future scenarios and a sense of apprehension about what was going to happen. According to the figures in the redundancy calculator that Edward had shown them on a PowerPoint slide, she could last for three months and just about pay off her outstanding debts. She didn't think she had the mental resilience to cope with that stress.

'Are you joining us for food tonight?' Haylee asked.

'I feel exhausted by everything. I'm going to check in with my dad and Sam and get an early night, I think,' Rosie replied.

'You sure?' Haylee checked. 'Only we reckon the best way to cope with this weekend is to get pissed in the bar and try to forget it's happening.'

Rosie was in full agreement with this summary, but an evening fuelled by alcohol was out the question for her. She couldn't risk the medication and alcohol cocktail, much as getting drunk would allow her to forget the whole sorry situation for a while. The noise was unpleasant too, the chat and laughter assaulting her ears. She needed some silence and stillness.

As people split off into groups and went their separate ways, Rosie saw that James was chatting to a group of friends from his office and took the opportunity to escape back to her room. She called her father, had a brief, monosyllabic chat with Sam, then switched off her phone, lay down on the bed and went to sleep in the dusky half-light.

She was shaken out of sleep by a tap at the door, gentle and unsure. Although her curtains were still open, it was dark and disorienting. She reached for her phone. It was past eight o'clock. She'd been out for almost three hours – no wonder she was hungry.

The tapping at the door continued.

'Who is it?' she asked, her throat dry, the words sticking.

'It's James. Are you okay? I noticed you didn't go to the restaurant. Do you need anything?'

'One moment,' she replied. Her eyes felt like they were glued together, a strange sensation at that time of day. Rosie lifted herself off the bed and made for the mirror opposite. She wiped her eyes, shuffled her hair so it didn't look like she'd been dragged through a hedge and then walked to the door. She opened it slowly.

'Hi,' James said, smiling.

'Hi. I fell asleep,' she replied, dazzled by the lighting in the corridor.

'Do you want to sneak off somewhere quiet for some food? There's a small bar on the other side of the conference centre. We'll be able to get a bar meal there and avoid the riot that's taking place in the restaurant.'

'Is it bad?' Rosie asked.

'It's like the last supper. They all think they're losing their jobs, so they're doing the only thing possible: getting pissed on the company expense account. Only Edward reminded them all that the allowance under company policy is only £12. I'm not sure that £12 is enough to drown your sorrows without having to subsidise the path to oblivion with your own money. Most of them seem past caring.'

'It's that bad, is it?'

'What's worse is that Edward Logan is sitting on his own at a single table. If he wasn't such a complete dickhead, I might feel sorry for him.'

'Poor old Edward,' Rosie said, picturing him trying to maintain some dignity while the rest of the staff enjoyed a drink-fuelled riot on an adjacent table. 'Who'd go into HR as a job? You're supposed to be a friend, but you're always the enemy. You're meant to be caring and touchy-feely, but you're there to save the company as much money as possible. It's not a job I'd like.'

'HR are the cockroaches of the corporate world,' said James, like it was a subject he'd given some consideration to. 'They'll always be the last out of the building to turn off the lights.'

'I'll join you for that bar meal,' Rosie said, her stomach grumbling. 'I'll need to stick with Edward's £12 allowance though. From the sound of today's presentations, redundancy may be a little closer than I'd like.'

Rosie took ten minutes to freshen up so she didn't look like a woman who'd been asleep for three hours. Then she joined James out in the corridor at the pre-arranged time.

He'd already checked out the second bar, and they managed to get there without being spotted by any of their colleagues. It was just what Rosie needed – a companion to make the evening pass quicker, without the mayhem of a large, drunken group.

Having taken her drugs, she was feeling confident for the evening ahead. Whenever she was with James, her anxiety subsided. She liked that about him.

They ordered bar meals and Rosie decided to risk one small glass of wine. Taken with food, she saw no harm in it. James was easy company, and before long, he'd once again managed to charm her away from her dark thoughts and back to a world of simple pleasures and quiet enjoyment. He never asked her about her past. He seemed content to deal with her in her present. That felt refreshing after so much time spent raking over the dead, grey ashes of what came before.

The conversation was steady and fun, fuelled by the glue of shared office experiences. No corporate stone was left unturned as they demolished their meals and Rosie ventured a second glass of wine. After all, she was having fun; she deserved it, didn't she?

James did an uncanny impersonation of Annabelle Reece-Norton. He captured her posh voice and haughtiness perfectly. Much as Rosie loved Annabelle, she almost wet herself laughing when James mimicked her talking about her beloved horses, and she had to excuse herself to visit the toilet. James even laughed at her reference to her struggling pelvic floor muscles; most men would have squirmed at the mention of such an indignity.

As Rosie checked herself in the bathroom mirror, she thought about what she was doing. If she ordered a third glass of wine, she was committing to a dangerous course of action. The mixture of alcohol and medication could be explosive. She was as likely to sink back into depression as she was to be buoyed by the move.

Fuck it! she thought. *I deserve this.*

She re-joined James at the table. He looked pleased to see her, as if he was enjoying the evening as much as she was, almost as if it was a date. She felt like an adult again. It had been a long time coming.

'Hey, who's this?' James asked. 'Whatevva! I'm just an intern. It don't matter to me! You oldies are mingin', talk to the hand, why don't you?'

'Let me guess,' Rosie smiled. 'That's Mackenzie, isn't it?'

The laughter and conversation continued and before she knew it, the conference centre staff were closing up the bar. James and Rosie got up from the table and began to walk back to their rooms. Encouraged by the evening, Rosie even took out her phone and re-installed Facebook, anxious to see what everybody else had been up to in the main restaurant.

'There's bound to be some gossip. There always is when everybody gets together.'

She placed her phone back in her bag, leaving it to install in its own time. There could be no distractions; she had plans for James that night, encouraged by the third glass of wine and a craving for close, physical contact.

As they arrived at the doors to their rooms, Rosie made her move.

'I've enjoyed this evening,' she said, nervous and out of practice at making an advance. 'Would you like to come in for coffee or something?'

She knew she must be blushing as she blundered through her words, but she was certain James liked her and even if they just kissed, that would be fine; it was a start.

James' face blanched, he looked immediately uncomfortable.

'Oh, Rosie, I wasn't after that. I enjoy your company...'

'Oh no, I meant to come in for a coffee, really, that's all I was suggesting.'

'I'm sorry Rosie, I'm tired, I think we're probably best calling it a night.'

'Yes, of course, more boring nonsense from Edward tomorrow. Thanks for this evening.'

'Yes, thanks. I enjoyed it, really I did.'

They entered their respective rooms in synchronised awkwardness. How could she have got it so wrong? Rosie was sure that James was flirting with her. Was she so out of practice that she'd lost her ability to read the situation?

She felt drunk and emotional. It was probably the medication. She'd been prepared to go all the way with James that night. How could she have been so clumsy?

Rosie pulled her phone out, anxious for a distraction. The Facebook app had completed its installation process, and she felt bold enough to risk it again and take a look. Besides, there was bound to be some work-related chit-chat on there to take her mind off what just happened out in the corridor.

She logged in and waited for the notifications to appear, anxious in case there were any more disturbing images. The moment she saw that she had five new notifications, she knew she should have stopped. But like a fly heading towards a UV light in a kitchen, she couldn't help herself.

Uninstalling Facebook on her phone hadn't stopped the messages coming; it only meant she hadn't seen them. There were four more dickpics, sent on different days during the past week. And there was a new image too, sent only ten minutes previously. It showed her and James sitting at a table in the bar, laughing.

Someone had been there, watching them – presumably the same person that had photographed them in the bar of the pub and sent the Chucky doll and the pornographic images. They were there at the conference centre – Rosie had probably spoken to them that very day.

CHAPTER TWENTY

The light was fading, but Rosie made it back in time to pay her weekly visit to Liam's grave. It helped her to feel that the weekend hadn't totally been written off on work-related activities - it was a little oasis of personal time snatched at the end of a Sunday afternoon.

Iain and Sam were away walking in the park. They'd all travelled together on the tube, and Rosie had agreed to meet them at the park's tea room half an hour before closing time. She'd got back home just after one o'clock.

The working weekend had finished early after events took a turn and things became rebellious. Neil Jennings had consulted David Willis from his hospital bed. There was a strong feeling that there was a potential legal case in the offing, with Silverline Supply Chains having breached some of the terms of the buying-out contract. Rosie didn't quite catch the detail of it all, but the upshot was, the staff were mobilising, and there was a possibility that the fat lady might not yet have sung.

Rosie looked around the cemetery and made sure there was

nobody about. She liked to speak aloud to Liam – like they used to chat in the kitchen – but she didn't want anybody hearing her and thinking she was crazy. It had occurred to her once while sitting on the tube that if she just plugged some earphones in, most people would assume she was chatting to somebody on the phone, rather than sharing her thoughts with a man who'd been dead for two years. If only she could shake off her irrational paranoia that the social workers were following her, making sure she was capable of looking after her child.

'Hi Liam, sorry I'm late,' she began, once she was confident she was alone. His picture had been re-attached to the front of his headstone. Thank goodness her dad had managed to get it sorted out with the stonemason while she'd been at work. She sat on the wooden bench just beneath the cherry tree to the side of her husband's grave. It would bloom again soon, leaving a spectacular blizzard of pink blossom across the peaked earth beneath which Liam was buried.

Rosie liked to imagine that he was still there with her. He'd have loved the blossom.

She thought through the events of the weekend, especially how she'd embarrassed herself in front of James, even though he'd been terrific about it afterwards, reassuring her that he liked her a lot, but he wasn't ready for that kind of relationship again just yet.

It was a good thing that he'd knocked her back in the cold light of day; nothing good was likely to come from sleeping with a work colleague who she barely knew. She'd drunk too much, letting her loneliness get the better of her. Since Liam's death, she craved the familiar company of her husband. She could talk to her father, to Vera, even to Sam and Leone. But none of them gave her the intimate adult companionship that Liam had done. She missed it desperately.

'I think I'm ready to start a new relationship,' she said aloud as if trying on the idea for size. 'You know you'll always be my number one guy, but you buggered off, Liam, you left me. I think it's time now.'

She waited as if he were going to reply. They used to talk about what they would do if one of them died. They'd joke about it, assuming they had the luxury of a lifetime ahead of them.

'Just throw me in the wheelie bin,' he'd said to her. 'Now I think about it, don't do that – the council workers won't take me away, as I don't qualify as domestic waste. It'll require a special collection for a dead body.'

'Well, make sure you spend a decent period in mourning for me,' Rosie had said with a laugh, 'then get yourself another woman and go and have some fun with the life insurance money.'

They'd been organised and sorted out the life insurance; if only they'd taken as much care with car insurance. If Liam had drunk a few mouthfuls less, she wouldn't have been left high and dry.

'Of course, I'll be careful,' she continued. 'I'll make sure whoever it is cares for Sam as much as we... as much as I do, and I'll make sure he's safe. But it's time now, I think. It's been two years, that's long enough. I'm lonely, Liam, I'm just so lonely.'

Rosie began to cry, the tears dripping onto her shoes. She stood up, annoyed with herself for getting upset. She'd wanted to be strong; this conversation with her husband's ghost was all about moving on.

She walked over to the tap at the end of Liam's row of graves, picked up the metal bucket that had been left there by the council, and filled it with water. She'd brought an old rag with her. Liam's grave was showing signs of weathering, and she was keen to wash it down, to remove the lichen that had begun to form on it.

She knelt and ran her fingers over the engraving.

Liam Gary Taylor, beloved husband of Rosie, caring father of Sam and Phoebe (deceased).

The irony was that Liam had never known his children; he never got to meet them. When he was alive, he'd been desperate for them to be born, but he never got to witness that pleasure.

Rosie dipped the rag into the water, squeezed it out and wiped the front of the stone. The lichen had not yet grabbed a proper hold; thankfully it came off quickly. She checked that the plate holding her husband's photograph had been securely re-attached. Yes, it was firmly in place now.

Rosie looked around again, unable to shake the feeling that she was being watched, still unsettled by the photograph of her and James eating food together at the conference centre. If she didn't control her thoughts, they would spiral out of control. It was bad enough thinking the social care department had people tailing her, but the photos were real.

'Who's doing this?' Rosie asked, as if Liam had the answer. 'Why would someone be trying to freak me out like this? Every time I try to pull myself out of a hole, something comes to knock me back in again. I don't think I can take much more, Liam.'

Rosie washed the edges of the stone, then stood up, picked the bucket up by the handle, and moved to the other side of the grave. When she saw what had been taped to the reverse of the headstone, she dropped the bucket. The water seeped into the grass, forming a small puddle of drenched soil at her feet.

A series of pornographic pictures, taken from the same sort of magazine as the pages stuck on Leone's car, had been taped securely to the stone. She looked at the grave to the right of Liam's, then to the left, irrationally hoping that maybe somehow, this was a general act of vandalism rather than something that was specifically aimed at her.

Rosie felt the walls of her life caving in on her. It wasn't just the pressure of returning to work, the threat of losing her only source of income or the dysfunctional workplace she'd been forced to return to. It was the succession of unnerving events – the rat in the drawer, the late delivery through the letterbox, the mystery images on Facebook and now these pornographic magazine pages, lying in wait for her where she least expected it. Whoever it was had chosen places that were personal and private to her – her husband's grave and her own home.

Rosie tore the pictures off the headstone, screwing them up and throwing them on the ground. Then she screamed a very long scream of fear, frustration and despair.

CHAPTER TWENTY-ONE

Rosie was interrupted by the sound of her phone, the distinctive ring tone that she'd set to identify when Iain was calling. She sat down on the bench and collected her thoughts.

'Hi, Dad,' she said, accepting the call, trying her best to sound bright.

'Hi, is that Rosie?'

It was an unfamiliar voice. Rosie tensed.

'Who is this?'

'Rosie, are you driving or doing anything which may cause you to have an accident while taking this call?'

It was a female voice, definitely not somebody she knew.

'Who the hell is this? What's going on? Why do you have my dad's phone?'

'Rosie, I'm DI Sarah Fletcher. I need you to confirm that you're in a safe place while you take this call.'

'I am! Spit it out, what's going on? Is Sam okay? Has something happened to Dad?'

'Rosie, can I confirm that you are a relation of Iain's?'

'Yes, I'm his daughter. Please, tell me what the hell is going on.'

'This is the only number programmed into your father's mobile phone - that's why we're calling you. Your father has been the victim of an assault. The ambulance service rushed him to hospital.'

'Oh my god, is he alright? How badly is he hurt?'

'Try to stay calm, Rosie. He received a heavy blow to his head; he was found unconscious near some shrubs in Fountains Park. His face was badly bruised and paramedics were unable to give a prognosis at the scene. Where are you now Rosie? Can you come to the station?'

'Are you at the park? I'm just across the road. I can be there in five minutes if I run.'

'We're there now Rosie – you'll see us close to the bandstand. I'll look out for you.'

'What about Sam? Where's Sam? Is he okay?'

There was silence at the other end.

'Rosie, I need you to tell me calmly – who's Sam?'

'Sam is my son; he's two years old. He was in a pushchair. I was going to meet dad in the park.'

'Rosie, is there any chance your father might have left Sam somewhere safe?'

'No, he was looking after Sam. They were alone. He was taken, I know it. All this stuff that's been going on, some weirdo has snatched him. I thought it was me they were threatening, not my child.'

DI Fletcher's voice became muffled, as if she had her hand over the mouthpiece. It sounded like she was consulting her team. Then she spoke clearly again.

'Rosie, you have to join me in the park as soon as you can get here safely. I have several officers available, and I've just instructed them to begin a search of the park. Can you describe Sam to me, Rosie? Will I find a photograph of him on your father's phone?'

'No, my dad can barely work the phone, that's why mine is the only phone number programmed in. I'm not even sure it can take photographs. Sam is like any other two-year-old. He has freckles and dark hair. He's wearing a woolly, blue jacket with ladybird buttons. The pushchair is a three-wheeler – it has a black awning. There's a plastic steering wheel attached to one of the handles. Is that enough? Please find him.'

'We need to search the park before it gets dark. If you can come over here straight away, that will help consider-ably, Rosie. Please be careful. I'll be waiting for you. We're looking for Sam right now. I'll see you soon.'

Rosie ended the call. She hadn't realised, but the tears were still flowing. Who was this terrorising their lives? And why? What the hell had she done to deserve this?

She put her phone in her pocket and scanned the side paths of the cemetery to figure out the quickest way over to the park. It would be quicker to cross the busy main road if she used the exit closest to the crossing. She veered right, breaking into a run, desperate to get to the park, terrified for her dad and what might have happened to Sam.

Was this some pervert or child offender? Was this why she'd been getting all the pornographic images? Had it been a warning of what was to come?

She cursed herself for not having raised it with the police already. If she'd flagged it up straight away, this might never have happened. She'd never forgive herself if Sam had come to any harm.

Soon, she was at the crossing, amid the steady Sunday evening traffic. Most of the cars now had their sidelights on. The police would have to move fast if they were going to be able to find Sam in the light. If it became dark, whoever had him would disappear into the night.

She stood outside the grand Victorian stone entrance to the park, frantically trying to remember how to get to the bandstand. Taking a wrong turn would waste precious minutes. She glanced at every passer-by, wondering if they had hurt her father or if they were responsible for Sam going missing.

Her heart thumped angrily, protesting about the speed of her run from the cemetery. It pounded as if it was going to explode, but she had to push through it.

Think of Sam, she chanted to herself. *Sam needs you more than ever now.*

Far ahead, she saw a blue flashing light, a clue to where she was heading. She carried on running, even though her legs told her to rest and her chest burned with the pain. Soon she saw them: three police vehicles and an ambulance. A mature woman was there, not in a uniform, but wearing a fashionable coat and black boots. Was that DI Fletcher? She gave Rosie a look of recognition and began to walk up to her as if those few metres might make all the difference.

'Rosie?' she asked. 'What's your surname? Here, sit on this bench while you get your breath back.'

She placed her hand on Rosie's shoulder and guided her towards an ornate, metal seat. It was cold, but Rosie didn't care.

'It's Taylor,' she replied. 'Rosie Taylor.'

'Do you have any ID on you?' DI Fletcher asked, calm and measured.

Rosie felt in her pocket and took out her purse.

'Yes, what do you need? I've got a bank card. Here's my work ID, is that any good?'

She handed it to DI Fletcher who checked it and gave it back.

'That's great, Rosie, thank you. I hope you understand that we have to check.'

'Yes, yes, of course,' she replied, fighting to control her breathing. 'Now where's Sam? Please – have you found him yet?'

'I have officers searching the park.'

Rosie jumped up from the bench.

'I need to help them. We have to be out there looking for Sam.'

'Rosie, you must stay calm. That's the best thing you can do to help your son. We're searching the park now, and if he's here, we'll find him. I need you to answer some questions first. That will give us the best chance.'

If Rosie could have turned into a gust of wind and blown through all four corners of the park in a moment, searching for her son, she would have. She wanted to be everywhere at once, but she was already exhausted from her run. It was best to sit for a moment.

The ambulance pulled away. Her dad... oh God, she hadn't even asked about him. 'Is Dad ok?'

DI Fletcher looked like she was steeling herself. She waited for Rosie to calm and settle.

'He's in good hands - the paramedics know what they're doing. Is there any chance that your father could be becoming forgetful, Rosie? Might he have left Sam somewhere?'

'No, he's still sharp as a tack, my dad. He wouldn't have forgotten Sam. I would have noticed if that was happening, wouldn't I?'

She thought about her father. He was walking more slowly and his voice had become reedier since her car accident, but that was down to growing old, wasn't it? She couldn't remember what she'd done five minutes ago, so how would she spot if her father was in the early stages of dementia? Is that what the DI was suggesting?

'Rosie, I need to ask you some delicate questions now. I want you to know that we're making a detailed search, so if he's in this park, we'll find him.'

'You know already, don't you?' she asked.

DI Fletcher nodded.

'We know that you've been struggling with your mental health, Rosie. Your records show that social care raised concerns about the safety of Sam. We also know that you didn't want your father to become Sam's ward while you were ill. I'm not suggesting anything, Rosie. But you do understand that I have to ask, don't you?'

It always came back to this. Every time Rosie tried to claw her way out of the pit, they pulled her back down again.

'I would never harm my son,' she said, her words precise and controlled.

'I know you'd never do it intentionally, Rosie. But mental illness can be a complex issue. Sometimes it can make us do things which are not in our nature.'

'I did not harm Sam. I was in the cemetery at the time, visiting my husband's grave.'

'Did you attack your father, Rosie? I have to ask.'

'No! I love my dad,' she protested. 'I would never hurt him. And the only reason I didn't want him to become Sam's ward is that I felt so damned ashamed. I felt such a miserable failure as a mother.'

She was trying to hold back her tears, but she couldn't stop them. She wanted to be in control like DI Fletcher, but the torrent of emotions rioting through her body prevented that.

A police officer, dressed in uniform, had approached them from behind. Rosie hadn't noticed until she was dimly aware of somebody hovering to her side. It looked like he'd been keeping his distance, waiting to get the nod from the DI to approach.

'What is it?' DI Fletcher asked, 'Do we have any news about Sam?'

The police officer was concealing something in his hand. He held it out towards them.

'We found this near the boating lake,' he began. 'Does it belong to your child, madam?'

It was a plastic steering wheel which looked like somebody had stamped on it and attempted to smash it. Rosie recognised it immediately as Sam's.

CHAPTER TWENTY-TWO

Rosie recognised the signs before she admitted them to herself. She was blanking things out again, which she hadn't done for months. DI Fletcher had reassured her that discovering the broken toy didn't mean any harm had come to Sam. She also recalled how DI Fletcher had put her arm around her and held her firmly as she sobbed. And she had a vague memory of being asked if she needed to take any medication or if there was somebody she could call.

When Rosie drifted back into the present once again, it was as if she'd had an out-of-body experience and was waking from a bad dream; the fear, the terror and the sweat were all there. But when she looked around her, all she could see was a park gradually fading into the darkness of night and a police officer who seemed out of his depth.

'There's nothing we can do here for the time being, Rosie. Why don't I run you over to the hospital to see your dad? How does that sound?'

The DI's steady voice served as a bridge from Rosie's fraying mind to the present.

'What about Sam? I can't leave Sam.'

'The moment they find him, I'll let you know.'

'Are you sure? Shouldn't we be helping or something?'

'The best thing we can do right now is to stay calm and be ready. Is there anybody you want to call, Rosie? Let me take you to your dad. We'll know the moment that Sam is found, I promise you.'

'Do you think they'll find him? Will he be alive?'

Every time she thought about it, Rosie felt her sanity slipping away. She needed to hang on, to stay with DI Fletcher, for Sam's sake. She couldn't drift away, even though oblivion was beckoning her now.

'I'll call Vera,' she said, fumbling for her phone.

'Who's Vera?' DI Fletcher asked. 'Is she family?'

'No, she's the psychiatric nurse who helped me to get well again,' Rosie replied. 'She knows how to help me. She knows what to do.'

The dial tone sounded, but there was no answer and no voice mail either.

'Damn it!' Rosie cursed.

'It's okay,' DI Fletcher said. 'My car is parked up just behind the bandstand. Let's go and see how your father is doing. If they find Sam, they'll bring him to the hospital to give him a check-up. We'll be in the right place.'

Rosie stood up and waited for the DI to guide her. It reminded of her of Trinity Heights when Vera would give her the medication, and she'd be completely compliant, waiting to be told what to do.

If there was one big advantage to living in London, it was that everything was clustered close together. The Sunday traffic was conducive to a fast drive, and they were at the reception desk of the hospital in no time. Rosie was accustomed to the clinical nature of the decor, and the crisp pressed linen of the nurse's uniforms. She wanted to sink into it and allow the caring arms of the medical profession to take her in and soothe away all her troubles.

DI Fletcher took the lead, looking like she'd done this a million times before. She flashed her ID, checked Iain's full name and date of birth with Rosie and noted the ward number and wing details. She strode confidently through the corridors as if she'd memorised every inch of the medical labyrinth. The signage pointed the direction like a hypochondriac's almanac, listing every possible problem that a human being might suffer: oncology, renal, cardiology and orthopaedic. It was a Who's Who of things that might kill you. They were heading for Neurology; Rosie knew that could mean brain damage and it wasn't good.

'They're taking your dad for a scan,' DI Fletcher updated her. 'They're still not entirely certain whether he fell or was struck from behind.'

'Is he going to die?' Rosie asked. 'Is my dad going to make it?'

She thought of how she would cope if he died. She couldn't face visiting another grave up at the cemetery. They were on rotation now; Liam and Phoebe got weekly visits and her mum was relegated to once-monthly. It was a large cemetery; her mum's grave was on the far side, well away from Phoebe and Liam.

She had to believe that Sam would be okay, because it was unbearable to contemplate her son coming to any harm. Rosie had been to some desolate places, but the idea of losing a second child was beyond darkness; it was the abyss.

She took a chair in the waiting area, and DI Fletcher brought her a plastic cup filled with soup. It reminded her of going swimming as a child. She'd be sitting there, her hair still wet while her dad bought a packet of crisps from the machine and a hot drink of her choice. She always chose the soup. It reminded her of family for some reason.

'We need to think ahead to tonight,' DI Fletcher said quietly, after taking a sip of her black coffee. 'Is there anybody who can stay with you if we don't find Sam?'

Rosie was embarrassed to answer that question. Her father was it. If he was out of the picture, she had nobody that she could rely on. Sure, she knew people at work; Haylee, Annabelle, even James. But they were colleagues, not friends. Friends had been in short supply while she'd been in Trinity Heights.

'I'll be okay on my own,' she replied. 'I'll call my friend Leone – she'll come round if I need her.'

Rosie reached for her phone. She still had the pictures on it. Perhaps she should show them to DI Fletcher? She navigated to Facebook, her thumb working away on the small screen. There were no new messages.

She tapped the bell icon to open up her notifications. That couldn't be right – there were no images from the profile with James' name on it. She scrolled down, making sure she hadn't done anything stupid. It wasn't as if she got many notifications. There was nothing there. Had the person deleted the account? Would that remove the notifications? Or had she imagined it? She cursed herself for not downloading the images onto the device, but that would have been stupid – she never wanted to see those horrible pictures ever again.

A doctor walked up to them, a clipboard in hand. It was such a hackneyed image, but it primed her for what was coming.

'Ms Taylor, DI Fletcher,' he held out his hand to be shaken by each of the women. Rosie noticed it was wet and clammy. She hoped that wasn't because he was about to deliver bad news.

'Mr Ingram is in a stable condition, but we've induced a temporary coma, for his welfare.'

'Will he die?' Rosie asked. She dreaded the answer. If he died, it would be game over. She couldn't navigate her way through another bereavement.

'I don't think so,' the doctor replied. 'We are concerned about potential brain damage, and there are signs that your father is in the early stages of dementia. We'll have a clearer picture tomorrow morning. It's always quiet around here on a Sunday, as I'm sure you can imagine.'

'Can I see him?' Rosie asked.

The doctor nodded.

'Yes, but only briefly. He needs rest and care right now. He's in the best place, Ms Taylor. We'll take good care of him.'

Rosie drifted after that, eventually finding herself in the car, only vaguely recalling Iain hooked up to the monitors amid the steady beeps of the medical equipment that confirmed he was still alive.

DI Fletcher was saying something to her, but she didn't retain much of it. Was the detective hanging around because she was terrified she might do something stupid if left alone? She would never do anything stupid while Sam was alive. If he was dead, she couldn't offer the same assurance. They might be burying them together if her boy came back to her dead.

'You've got my direct phone number. I mean it, Rosie – if you need to speak to me, don't hesitate to call. I've also given you the telephone number for the police station, the direct line to your father's ward and The Samaritans' number, just in case you need it. If I hear anything – and I mean anything – about Sam, I will contact you straight away. I won't wait, I'll pass on any news to you immediately. Keep your phone charged, Rosie and make sure you have the ring tone on.'

She kissed Rosie on the forehead. It was an unusual but kind thing to do. DI Fletcher was trying to show Rosie that she cared; it was more than just another job. Rosie appreciated that more than DI Fletcher would probably ever know.

The moment the door was closed, Rosie made sure that it was securely locked, then headed for the kitchen cupboard at the end of the units. Inside were large pharmaceutical bags packed with her medical supplies for that month. Rosie knew precisely how she would get through that night. She began to peel the pills from their foil enclosures. This was how she blotted out the pain.

CHAPTER TWENTY-THREE

'My fucking neighbour!' was the first thought that went through Rosie's mind as her eyes pulled into focus, and she recognised the distinctive interior paintwork of Trinity Heights.

'Hi, Rosie, I've got good news for you.'

It was DI Fletcher's voice. Rosie checked again. This wasn't her bedroom. It was one of the rooms at the psychiatric hospital. What the hell had happened? She hadn't intended to kill herself. She just wanted to sleep. It took her a moment to gain control of her speech.

'How did I get here?' Rosie asked.

'We sent an officer round last night, but you wouldn't answer the door. We had to break it down. You've got one hell of a nosey neighbour. She was out in her nightgown and slippers, making all sorts of ridiculous claims about you. I ignored her, just for the record. Anyway, I've got good news. We found Sam.'

'Where? Is he safe? Where did you find him?'

Rosie sat upright in the bed, desperate for news.

'He was found in a nearby pub. Someone had just left

him there. He was perfectly safe – he'd been there for two hours, and nobody had even noticed. They'd all assumed he belonged to somebody else. He slept through the entire thing, according to the locals.'

'I can't believe it! Who took him? Was he there all the time?'

Rosie felt a wave of relief wash over her, rinsing away the dark thoughts of the previous night.

'There was no CCTV in the pub – it was very spit and sawdust, I'm afraid. Nobody had any recollection of who brought Sam in. It could be anybody, Rosie. But he's safe, don't worry, he's been checked over, and he came to no harm.'

'Can I see him?' Rosie asked, desperate now to be sure that DI Fletcher wasn't lying to her.

'He's over in Paediatrics, just while they make sure everything is fine. Now, I don't want you to worry, but he has a member of the council's social care team with him.'

'Those bastards are not taking him away from me,' Rosie began, the anger igniting instantly.

'Rosie, it's fine. We brought you here as a precaution. You can leave whenever you want.'

'They're not sectioning me?' Rosie asked.

'No, it's fine, Rosie. You can walk out of here whenever you're ready. I was first to see you in your bedroom. You know you took too many sleeping pills last night, don't you?'

'It was an accident.'

DI Fletcher softened her voice.

'Rosie, it's okay, I won't tell anybody. I've experienced a nervous breakdown myself in the past. It's so hard fending off all the questions about your commitment to the job and how you square looking after your kids with a job, especially one like mine. I get it, Rosie. Sometimes you need to shut off your mind. I'd have done the same if one of my kids went missing. But promise me, when you're back at home safe with Sam, promise me you'll take the help that's on offer here. You don't have to go through it on your own. It's going to be even harder, with your dad needing some time to recover. Ask for help, Rosie, please. Don't let it drown you.'

DI Fletcher put her hand on top of Rosie's and gave it a gentle squeeze.

'How's my dad – any news yet?' Rosie asked.

'I checked for you first thing this morning. He's stable. They're talking about bringing him out of the coma today. There's no brain damage, that's the good news. But he was struck on the head, Rosie. Is there anybody who might do that to your father?'

Rosie's mind started to race. For a split second, she considered sharing everything with DI Fletcher. She genuinely seemed concerned. But how could she prove it? The pictures sent on Facebook had gone, the mystery account now deleted. The rat in her desk drawer at work would be written off as bad luck. She'd thrown away the pornographic magazine pages and the Chucky doll had been taken away in the last bin collection.

If she shared all that information with DI Fletcher, they'd have her committed. It would be seen as the paranoid delusions of a woman with a history of mental illness; they'd lock her up and throw away the key. And with Iain in the neurological unit – showing early signs of dementia too – what the hell was she going to do? If she ended up in Trinity Heights, there was nobody to care for Sam; he'd go into care, raised by the state. She would be sentencing her son to a life of estrangement, rootlessness and abandonment.

DI Fletcher filled the silence.

'We think it was a random attack,' she said. 'We're mystified as to why they didn't take your father's wallet or phone, but it does look like he was struck from behind. A bloodied stone was found discarded in a bush in the park this morning. It was close to where your dad was discovered. We also don't know why somebody would take Sam like that. Perhaps it was your father they were after; maybe they were struck by guilt and decided to leave him somewhere safe. I don't think we'll ever know, Rosie, not unless your dad saw something. But at least Sam is safe now.'

'Yes, I'm so grateful for that,' Rosie replied.

'Oh, you've had some chap called Edward Logan calling you all morning on your mobile phone. I answered it in the end and told him what had happened. What a strange man he is.'

'What did you tell him?' Rosie asked.

'Well, nothing, I have an obligation of confidentiality. I just thought I'd better answer the phone and put him out of his misery. He called eleven times between nine and ten o'clock. Do you owe him money or something?'

'Blood more like,' Rosie replied.

DI Fletcher smiled. 'I told him you wouldn't be in for work today due to a family emergency. You can fill in the gaps however you please. By the way, you need to put a pin code on that phone of yours. There was no security on it, so I could just help myself to any information on there. It's a good job I'm one of the good guys!'

'Yeah, I know,' Rosie replied, a little sheepish at having been caught out. 'I'm not a big phone user. It's mainly for my dad to call me about Sam. I promise I'll get it sorted. Did Edward say anything else?'

'Well, it was all rather odd. He started explaining which form you'd need to fill in. I've never heard anything like it.

Just for the record, he wanted you to know that you need to complete a sick form if you're ill and a leave form if you're not. And if your absence doesn't fall into either of those two categories, you'll need to report to him immediately upon your return to work for a brief interview. What an unusual place of employment you have.'

'You can say that again,' Rosie agreed. 'So, am I free to go now? Can I pick up Sam?'

'Yes, you can go whenever you're ready. You're a voluntary patient. Please make sure you bring along full identification when you go to pick up Sam – like a passport and council tax documents, or they won't release him to you.'

Rosie's phone rang from the side of the bed. DI Fletcher picked it up, read the screen, then handed it to her.

'It's not that Edward guy again, don't worry. It's somebody called Leone, is that your friend?'

'Yes. I wonder what she's calling about,' Rosie said.

'I'll be on my way,' DI Fletcher mouthed as Rosie picked up the call. She put up her hand to acknowledge what the DI had done for her.

'Hi, Leone.'

'What the hell has been going on?' Leone asked. 'I drove past your house this morning, and the front door was boarded up. What on earth happened?'

Rosie brought her up to speed.

'Rosie, this isn't normal. If you need a witness to the Chucky doll, I'll happily help. You've got to tell the police what's going on.'

'They'll think I'm losing my mind again,' Rosie replied. 'Come on, Leone. You know how this works. Don't give them an inkling that you're struggling and everything will be okay. Show them any weakness, and you lose your child. You, of all people, know that.'

'There was some mail on the doorstep. Your letterbox is blocked by the sheet of chipboard that was nailed over it. I assume the postman left it there for you. Anyhow, it's safe, I've got it; you can have it when I next see you. Somebody looks like they've sent you a card for your dad already.'

'What do you mean?' Rosie asked, immediately tense. 'Nobody even knows about my dad yet. Open it, will you? What does it look like?'

'It's just a coloured envelope with a card inside.'

Rosie listened as she heard the sounds of Leone balancing her phone under her chin as she tore open the envelope.

'Oh,' was all she said.

Rosie didn't need to see the card to know who it was from.

'Tell me,' she instructed Leone. 'Don't protect me. I want to know what's in it.'

'There's a photograph of you. It looks like you're kneeling by a grave. What an odd photo to send. There's a message too.'

'Read it,' Rosie said.

'It says *Wishing Iain and Sam a speedy recovery. Take care, Rosie. It might be you next time.*'

'Does it have a postmark? Is there a signature?'

'Nothing,' Leone replied. 'That's it.'

Rosie felt the despair festering in the pit of her stomach. She sat in silence, Leone on the other end of the phone, neither of them knowing what to say.

Vera walked into the room as if nothing had happened.

'Hello trouble,' she said. 'Fancy seeing you in here again.'

CHAPTER TWENTY-FOUR

'You're the last person I expected to see here today,' Haylee said, a look of delight and surprise on her face. 'Are you okay? The way Edward described things, it sounded like whatever you were off work with was terminal.'

'It's not quite that bad, you'll be pleased to hear,' Rosie replied. 'I'm hoping James hasn't been out for lunch yet. Is he still in the office?'

'Yes, he's still here.'

'I need you to keep a secret for me, Haylee. I'm not coming into work just yet, but I need to see James without causing a big fuss. Can you ring through to his desk and ask him to meet me at the Costa Coffee store just up the road at half-past twelve?'

'This all sounds very cloak and dagger. Are you two getting it together?'

'Nothing like that.' Rosie forced a smile. 'But I do need to keep Edward off the scent, so I'd be grateful for your help.'

'No problem,' Haylee replied. 'You did the right thing throwing a sickie this morning. It's been terrible here today, as if someone's died. Nobody is talking to Edward after the weekend. You could cut the atmosphere with a knife.'

'I'll be back tomorrow,' Rosie replied. 'Please don't tell anyone I was here. You know what Edward is like – he'll have me making up my hours if he knows I can still walk and breathe.'

Haylee looked excited by the thought of conspiracy. The intrigue had probably made her day. Rosie had often wondered how Haylee's brain hadn't died putting phone calls through to the offices all day. She thanked her for her help and headed for the stairs, to avoid being spotted by any of her colleagues. Thirteen floors up – no wonder nobody ever used the staircase. At least the walk down would be a lot easier than the walk up had been. Her legs ached with the effort of it.

The sparse, concrete staircase echoed as she began her downwards journey. As she turned the corner onto the landing, she saw Mackenzie, smoking a cigarette. Rosie hadn't come dressed for the workplace. She was wearing the same trainers as when Sam was snatched the day before, having come in a taxi directly from Trinity Heights.

Mackenzie hadn't seen or heard her. Placed on the floor at her side was a white paper bag, a packet of crisps and a can of Fanta.

Rosie felt like a naturalist who'd just spotted a rare creature that was utterly unaware it was being observed. She stood completely still and silent as Mackenzie took a drag on the cigarette and defiantly blew the smoke out of her mouth. Then she stubbed out the cigarette on the floor, pushed it with her foot into the corner and popped a mint in her mouth. She stooped down to pick up the paper bag, unfolded the end of it, removed the sandwich that was contained within it, lifted the top slice of bread, then spat in it. Rosie knew immediately who that sandwich was for.

She stood completely still, wondering whether she should let Mackenzie know that she was there. She didn't have much choice. It was almost midday. The staff would be teeming out into the lifts shortly. She would be unable to leave the building without being spotted. Besides, she'd just figured out the final part of her plan, and it suited her to have Mackenzie owing her a favour.

'Wouldn't you be better putting mayo on that?' she said.

Mackenzie turned around immediately with a look of shock.

'How long have you been there?' she asked.

'Long enough to see you spitting into Edward's sandwich.'

She waited to see how Mackenzie would respond. Fight or flight?

'Well, he's a right tosser anyway,' she said. It looked like it was going to be the fight option. 'Don't tell me you wouldn't cough all over his food, given half the chance.'

Rosie thanked her lucky stars that Mackenzie had found work experience at a supply chain company rather than a local eatery; she was much less of a hazard in an office environment.

'What are you doing lurking in the stairwell?' Mackenzie asked.

'I won't tell if you don't,' she said. 'There's not a person in that office who wouldn't want to put much worse in Edward's sandwich.'

'I thought you were away today?' Mackenzie interrupted. 'Something about a family drama, Edward said.'

Rosie needed to cover her tracks, especially as the first

person Mackenzie would be heading for on her return to the office was Edward.

'Can you keep a secret, Mackenzie?' Rosie said. She was playing with fire, but she had to take the chance. 'I was sneaking by to drop some paperwork in with Haylee. I didn't want to get caught in the office after the weekend. You know what a dick Edward can be. I'll keep quiet about the extra ingredient in his sandwich. Oh, by the way, smoking on the premises is a sackable offence too – Edward would have a field day if he knew about that.'

Mackenzie almost managed a smile.

'It makes the cigarettes taste twice as good, knowing what that idiot would say,' she replied. 'Don't worry. I won't say anything. I hate this shitty apprenticeship, but it's better than anything else that's on offer at the moment.'

Rosie decided to make her move. To get ahead of her current problems, she would need Mackenzie's help. She studied the teenager for a while, deciding if she was about to do the right thing. Mackenzie was young and a bit tactless, but she was friendly enough and didn't mean anybody any harm. Sure, she'd spat in Edward's sandwich, but Rosie probably would have done the same thing at that age.

'You know you offered to babysit for me?' she began, still uncertain she was making the right call.

Mackenzie was the last person she wanted to leave Sam with, but bearing in mind he'd been partially abducted the day before, it seemed to be the least of her problems.

Mackenzie looked up at her, with a look of mild interest on her face.

'Could you do a two-hour trial for me this evening? I'll pay you.'

'How much?'

Rosie was heartened to see that job satisfaction played a crucial factor in Mackenzie's decision-making process.

'Five pounds an hour.'

'Done! That's more than I get paid here. What time do you want me there?'

'Is seven o'clock okay? I'll pay your tube fare as well. You know where I live already, I take it?'

Mackenzie had the decency to display at least a little shame.

'Yeah, I look up all the staff on Google Maps to see where they live. It's boring otherwise. Your house is nice.'

Rosie felt a small shiver running through her body. Nothing was private any more – a teenager like Mackenzie could do everything but peer through her bedroom window via her computer. What else had she been up to while she was moving files around the office?

'So, seven o'clock, Mackenzie. Please do your best to get there on time. I'll see you later.'

Rosie would not typically have chosen the surly teenager as her partner in crime, but the opportunity had arisen, and it allowed her to place the final piece in her plan. The remainder depended upon James. Mackenzie was sensible enough to hold down an apprenticeship, she'd be responsible enough to care for Sam for two hours in the safety of his own home.

The half an hour it took to nurse a cup of coffee before James arrived at the Costa store seemed interminable. Rosie was on edge, doing her best to keep everything together. She was desperate to see Sam, but she had to take this detour first, to put things in place. Whoever was making her life hell, whoever it was who'd threatened Sam, she had to get the evidence and take it to DI Fletcher. Without that, they'd think she was going crazy. At least James believed her. He would help.

'Hey, Rosie! I didn't expect to see you here today after the email Edward sent out. I knew something was up when Haylee said you were in Costa.'

He'd brought her over a coffee, the same way she'd had it at the conference centre. She liked his attention to the small details.

'Yes, I know it's a bit of a hike from the office, but I didn't want to risk seeing anybody from work. You'll keep this quiet, won't you?'

'Yes, of course. I'm intrigued by why you want to see me, to be honest.'

'You know all these weird things that have been going on? You know about the horrible photos already, because I accused you of sending them.'

'Thanks for reminding me about that,' James said, giving her a wry smile.

'There's more to it,' Rosie continued, finding her confidence. 'Someone has been sending pornographic images. My husband's grave has been attacked. A horrible doll was sent to Sam on his birthday.'

'Damn it, Rosie - you've kept all this to yourself? I'm glad you trust me enough to share this stuff.'

'That's why I want your help,' Rosie replied. 'I have to put an end to this, but I need evidence. I'm sure I know who's responsible. It's been driving me crazy thinking about it.'

'Who?' James asked.

'Who else?' Rosie said. 'Edward Logan. He's the only suspect. He knows about my past problems, he has access to my personnel file and he knows my home address. You said yourself he's visited your house on more than one occasion.

He's been inappropriate and threatening at work – not just with me. It has to be Edward. I'll bet he was responsible for that rat, too. He's trying to squeeze me out, I'm certain of it.'

'I know HR people can be guilty of sharp practice at times, but surely not?'

'How would you describe Edward Logan in one word?' Rosie challenged.

'Weird?' James replied. 'Unusual. Unsettling. Strange. Not of this world. Do you want any more?'

'Weird, that's it. That's how we'd all describe him. That man's not right. He's been trying to intimidate me, and I've got a plan to prove it. But I need your help—'

'I had a feeling that's why you asked me here. Go on then, how do you want me to help you?'

Rosie looked at him and, just as she'd done with Mackenzie earlier, she took a chance on her colleague. It was the only way she could put a stop to what Edward was doing. He was terrorising her. The man was a monster.

'We're breaking into his office. And we're doing it tonight.'

CHAPTER TWENTY-FIVE

It was a long time since Rosie had stayed at work after hours; she'd had to ask James to check up on the latest procedure for getting in and out at that time of night. Fortunately for her, many offices in London barely slept – if at all – so 24-hour access was a standard requirement for the busy, city workplace.

It had tortured her, not going to pick up Sam directly after leaving Trinity Heights, but she had to make the detour to meet with James first. She felt like an unfit mother, leaving her child in the care of the social worker like that, but with her father out of action in the same hospital, once she picked up her son, her hands were tied. She had a plan to reveal her tormentor, and if it worked, she'd be able to hand over some compelling evidence to DI Fletcher the following day. This would be solid evidence too, not the sort that made her look like she was paranoid.

After plotting with James, Rosie took an Uber directly back to the hospital, where she rushed in to pick up Sam. She gritted her teeth as she went through a humiliating series of security checks, including a call to Trinity Heights to confirm that she'd voluntarily discharged herself, rather than absconding. At last they handed Sam back to her.

He looked none the worse after his adventure the day before. They'd taken his pushchair with him to the hospital, and the only evidence that he'd ever been gone at all was the broken arm of the toy steering wheel which looked like it had been wrenched off.

Rosie walked along the hospital corridors, tracing her way to the neurological department where her father was being looked after. He was still in a coma. The police had been round checking, no doubt hoping to catch the scent of the person who'd attacked him. She kissed Iain and left him to the medical professionals. The next time she saw him, she was determined her life would be different.

Leone had been right about her front door; there was a note stuck on the chipboard which told her to call on her neighbour for access to the new key.

'I see you've been at it again,' her neighbour scolded. 'It frightened the life out of me when they battered your door down last night. That poor child of yours – it's a wonder he looks so calm.'

Rosie's neighbour made sure that she extracted her pound of flesh before handing over the key that the lock-smiths had left with her. Much as Rosie hated to admit it, it was the safest and best option, bearing in mind the treatment her front door had been subjected to. And she had to admit that if her next-door neighbour's door had been smashed in, she too would have complained about the neighbourhood going downhill.

She spent the afternoon playing with Sam, ignoring three calls from Edward Logan. He might turn up at the house to check up on her, but she'd have to take that risk. She was setting a trap to catch a rat. How ironic.

She'd felt queasy and light-headed since going into work and meeting James. Was she up to the night's escapades? The events of the past twenty-four hours had taken a heavy toll on her. Taking the extra sleeping pills the night before had probably not been such a bright idea.

Rosie made sure that she was up-to-date with her medication; she couldn't afford a panic attack while carrying out the plan she and James had agreed.

Mackenzie was early. She didn't relish having the teenager in her house, but Leone wasn't available that evening, and at least Mackenzie had shown some enthusiasm for the job.

'I came straight here from work,' she said as she looked at the door. 'Hell, this is a rough area if you've had yer door patched up like that.'

Sam lit up when he saw her, as if they were best buddies already. Mackenzie wasted no time; within seconds she was on the floor beside Sam, joining him at his playing.

'You're a natural,' Rosie commented. 'Maybe supply chains aren't your thing, Mackenzie. Have you ever thought about working with children?'

'Yeah, I love kids,' she replied. She had gum in her mouth again, and Rosie had to stop herself from worrying that it might end up stuck underneath the kitchen table. 'But you can't work with kids when... Let's put it this way: people aren't falling over themselves to employ a person like me.'

Rosie didn't force the issue, assuming that she meant people were put off by her physical appearance. If there was one thing she tried hard not to do, it was judging people by appearances alone. She knew that the way Mackenzie looked was not out of place among her own generation. And Sam liked her a lot, she was immediately comfortable messing around with him. What else did she need to know for an absence of no more than two hours? She knew more about Mackenzie than she did the social worker who'd been with her son for more than half-a-day. And Sam really didn't care about the heavy make-up, piercings and hairstyle. As far as he was concerned, it was a new playmate.

'I'm off then,' Rosie said.

Sam started to giggle, and Rosie finally brushed her doubts aside. The baby decided it, if Mackenzie was good enough for Sam then she was good enough for Rosie.

The tube was quiet at that time in the evening, and James had texted her to confirm that the coast was clear. Edward had gone home with a pile of files and his laptop. He'd even paid James a rare compliment, congratulating him on working late and letting him know it wouldn't go unnoticed in the current job review.

Rosie and James had agreed; no emails, no phone calls from or to the work switchboard and no texts discussing what they were about to do. Whoever was taunting her with foul images and threatening deliveries to the house had done an excellent job of covering their tracks. And now she and James would be playing the same game.

James was ready for her when she arrived. Rosie buzzed him from the front entrance of the building. He let her in remotely from Haylee's console at the reception desk. She used the lift this time; the stairs had exhausted her earlier, and from the way she was feeling, drained and vague, there was no way she'd make it thirteen floors up.

James had a coffee waiting for her; he was nothing if not attentive, he'd made the drink just the way she liked it. She wondered again why he'd knocked her back the other night. He seemed interested, and he was giving out all the right signals.

'Okay, so I'm going to give Mike, the man who never retires, a call. Did you leave your keys in Edward's office like we discussed?'

James nodded.

'Yes, I dropped them under his desk when I told him I needed to work late. He was so pleased with me that I thought he was about to give me a commendation medal there and then. What a twerp!'

Rosie took a sip of coffee and picked up the handset of one of the office phones. She dialled 8 for maintenance services.

'Hi Mike, it's Rosie on floor 13. I know you'll be about to clock off, but we're in a bit of a fix up here. Can you bring up your keys for the offices? We need to get in to retrieve my colleague's house keys.'

'Did he fall for it?'

'Yes, he's on his way. As soon as he opens up Edward's office, call the emergency maintenance line from your mobile phone. I want him distracted.'

The plan worked well. Mike turned up with a long chain of keys which opened up every door on floor 13. Rosie pointed to James' key through the glass of Edward's office door, and Mike started searching for the correct key before she'd even finished her sentence.

'Strictly speaking, I should get you to sign for this, but I want to be home to catch the football on TV, so I'll let you off this time as I trust you. I'll need to monitor you going into the office though.'

Mike's mobile phone rang as they'd planned.

'Damn, I'm never going to get away at this rate.'

Rosie darted into Edward's office, grabbed James' key and moved towards the door.

'All done here!' she smiled, 'You'd best get that call.'

As Mike turned away to pick up the call, Rosie stuck a piece of card in between the door and the frame to stop it closing fully. James ended the call to Mike before he could answer it, then turned towards him and started talking, to distract him further. All it took was a bit of sports banter, and Mike completely forgot to check that Edward's door was secure.

By the time James got back from seeing Mike out of the building, Rosie had finished her coffee and was working her way through Edward's filing cabinets.

'He's gone – I saw him out the front door,' James confirmed. 'Have you found anything?'

'Not yet,' Rosie replied. 'They haven't moved the personnel files onto the computer system yet – at least, they still have the paper back-ups. Look, here's yours!'

James' face whitened.

'Don't read that,' he said. 'I'll die of embarrassment.'

'Don't worry. It's not yours I'm after. It's Edward's I want to look at. Here it is.'

She held up a blue file as if it were a trophy, then set it on his desk to start reading.

'Anything I can do?' James asked.

'Yes. Check for photo paper, his camera or any SD cards. He has a camera in here somewhere. He took my staff picture using it. See if he leaves his PC on overnight too; I want you to look at his search history and see what he's been ordering.'

'You know this all looks paranoid, don't you?' James said.

'It's made me paranoid,' Rosie replied.

'His PC is still on. I can't see anything in his search history. It's all boring stuff about HR and redundancies. What have you got?'

'There's nothing in here, just his career history,' Rosie said, looking over at James. 'It's as boring as the man himself. He does seem to move around a bit, though. He never sticks around in one place for very long. He's like a bad penny.'

They carried on with their respective tasks, then Rosie spoke again.

'That's interesting, there's another file got caught in Edward's. Damn, I feel strange, I think I'm still suffering from last night's sleeping pills. Have you got any of your coffee left? I feel like I could fall asleep on the spot.'

'Sorry, mine's all gone,' he replied.

They worked in silence for a few moments, James exploring Edward's drawers and Rosie reading the file. It had Mackenzie's name written on it, but the name had been changed from what was on the original file. There was an internal note from David Willis noting the reason for the change. *Mackenzie has requested to be known by her paternal surname as of 24/01.*

Rosie's eyes scanned the document, interested to see what her original name had been. *Philpot.* That was an unusual name. By coincidence, it was Vera's surname too. Rosie thought nothing of it. But there was a handwritten note paper-clipped to David's memo, and there was something about the writing that made Rosie go back and check. She'd seen that handwriting before – on her medical notes at Trinity Heights. It was Vera's handwriting.

Incredulous, she read the letter. It was nothing remarkable, just a confirmation that Vera was Mackenzie's mother and verification that her married name had been Devereux. Was this the paranoia again? How come Vera's daughter was working in the same company as her? That was too much of a coincidence, surely?

As Rosie stood there, reading the file, she saw how it all joined up. David Willis knew Vera from the visits to Trinity Heights after the accident. Of course, he'd have met Vera. She was always around the ward. They must have got talking while Rosie was spaced out and on her meds. That figured – she wasn't much of a conversationalist when she was sedated. So why hadn't Mackenzie thought to mention it to Rosie? She'd had plenty of opportunities.

As James finished searching Edward's drawers and declared him innocent of all allegations, Rosie realised that she'd got it wrong. Edward's only crime was one of being socially inept. It wasn't him who'd been taunting her.

Rosie was more concerned about Mackenzie Devereux – Mackenzie *Philpot* – the mysterious young woman who was currently looking after her only child.

CHAPTER TWENTY-SIX

'What are you doing?' James asked, looking up from Edward's desk.

'I'm calling Mackenzie,' Rosie replied, pulling her mobile phone out from her pocket like she was drawing a gun.

'You look poorly,' James told her. 'Why don't you sit down and I'll call Mackenzie for you? Do you want a glass of water from the kitchen?'

'No, I'm calling her,' Rosie insisted. 'But I would like that glass of water.'

She dialled her home phone number, kept only for her dad's convenience. He preferred the landline to his mobile and still used the same heavy telephone in his house that he'd had since she was a child. It was a miracle it was still working.

She listened anxiously as the dial tone sounded, letting it ring fifteen times – sufficient for even Mackenzie to realise what it was – before ending the call. After a moment's panic, she figured that Mackenzie probably didn't even know what a landline was. She pictured her wandering around the house, trying to work out where the alien sound was coming from.

James entered Edward's office with a glass of water.

'You look like you're over-heating,' he said. 'Are you sure you're okay?'

'I feel terrible,' Rosie replied. 'But it can wait. It's probably just the events of the last 24 hours catching up with me. Besides, I did take more sleeping pills than I should have last night. I think it's just my body telling me to stick to the recommended dose.'

She took the glass from James and sipped the water.

'That tastes pretty horrible,' she commented. 'The water quality in this part of the city is terrible, but thanks, I needed that.'

She gulped down the entire glass and placed it on Edward's desk.

'Any luck with Mackenzie?' James asked. 'Why do you need to call her?'

'Take a look at this,' said Rosie, picking up the papers.

As she held up Mackenzie's file, she realised that her mobile number would be on the personnel records. She hadn't thought to jot down that information before she exited the house, instead leaving her details scribbled on a sticky note in case Mackenzie needed to reach her in an emergency. She tapped the number into her phone, then handed James the file. As he studied it, she listened to the sound of Mackenzie's ringtone. It went to voicemail.

Hey, it's Mackenzie! If you insist on leaving a message, do it after the stupid beep sound. I probably won't call you back unless you're offering me money. Or a free holiday. Or if you're a looker.

'I don't see anything here,' James said, handing back the

file. 'Besides, I thought it was Edward you suspected was bothering you?'

'Not any more,' Rosie said, re-dialling Mackenzie's number. 'James, will you get an Uber to pick us up from the entrance? We're going back to my house. You can send the costs to me. It's urgent.'

'Are you sure?' James asked, a look of concern on his face. 'I'm confident everything is okay. If we look hard enough, I reckon we'll soon find some evidence about Edward.'

'No, I need to get back to the house. Mackenzie is not who she appears to be. I think she's the one who's been sending all these vile things to me. Get that Uber ordered, then help me tidy up Edward's office.'

Rosie was giving James instructions now, not asking him.

Mackenzie's phone had gone to voicemail a second time. She fought with the rapidly descending fog in her mind, knowing she had to stay sharp for Sam's sake. Then, as she picked up Mackenzie's file to place it back where she'd found it, a shiver ran through her body.

When Sam had seen Mackenzie back at the house, he'd welcomed her like they were old friends. He was a two-year-old and didn't care that much who he was playing with, so long as they were friendly with him. But his eyes had lit up when Mackenzie had come in, as if he knew her already. Was Mackenzie the person who'd taken him in the park? Was it Mackenzie who'd hurt her dad?

'Forget the files,' Rosie said, 'We're going. Is that Uber coming?'

'Yes, how soon do you want it?' James asked.

'Now!' Rosie shouted at him. 'Get it now!'

'Hadn't we better tidy up in here? Edward will know we've been in his office?'

'Fuck Edward!'

Rosie felt the fury rising in her like a burning fireball. She'd had enough. She was going to give Mackenzie a piece of her mind and then she would have a serious word with the strange guy from HR. It was time to take back control. If she could only shake off the terrible feeling of vagueness. It must be a reaction to the extra sleeping pills. She wouldn't be doing that again, however much she wanted to knock herself out.

James was acting as if events were running away from him. He fussed about the room, putting the files back in place, picking up the glass of water and checking that everything was where it had been. He was doing it all whilst messing about with his phone.

'Are you coming with me, James?' Rosie asked. 'I could use some moral support. Besides, she's such a mouthy bitch that I'm expecting her to turn nasty when I confront her.'

She couldn't figure this out. Why the hell hadn't Vera mentioned it?

Now James had cleared the room, he followed Rosie out, making sure the door was shut behind them.

'I hope we can get back home fast. That little cow is getting a piece of my mind.'

The Uber was waiting outside for them by the time they'd locked up the office and made their way down to the lobby in the lift.

The driver said nothing throughout the journey and she was grateful that he wasn't the chatty type. She didn't even speak to James, who seemed to be more interested in texting somebody. All she could think of was Mackenzie. Why didn't she know that Vera had a daughter?

She searched her mind, thinking back to her time in the hospital. It wasn't the most lucid period of her life. What did she know about Vera? Yes, she was divorced. Yes, she had mentioned that she had a daughter. But she called her Mack! Of course she had a daughter. She'd even been to the hospital. Rosie forced open the compartments of her mind. Mackenzie had long hair then, and it wasn't pink or shaved at that time. She didn't have piercings or make-up either. Two years ago, she was just like any other teenager.

She hadn't been around in the later stages of Rosie's recovery, though. Where had she gone? Damn, she'd known the girl all the time but hadn't realised. A buzz cut, a splash of hair dye, a couple of piercings and a different environment made all the difference. Why hadn't Mackenzie said something? Vera's Mack had to be MacKenzie. They were one and the same.

They soon arrived at the house; it was only a ten-minute journey at that time of night. She got out of the vehicle, leaving James to deal with the pleasantries. As she walked around the car, Rosie saw that the hallway light was on and the door was wide open. She knew straight away that something was up. How could she have been so blind to miss that it was Mackenzie who'd been tormenting her all along?

She rushed up the drive, stumbling as she did so, feeling drunk. Her head was spinning, but her fear for Sam drove her forward. As she ran up to the front door, she saw a body lying on the carpet. Paperwork was strewn across the floor, as if he'd had it in his hand when he'd fallen. There was a bloody patch at the back of his head, suggesting he'd been struck from behind as soon as he'd walked into the house.

'Edward?' she said, recognising his shoes immediately. He must have come to the house with some administrative work for her to complete. There was a form with the words

Sick Leave printed at the top; it now had splashes of blood across it.

Rosie ran into the house, her heart thudding. It was all falling into place: Mackenzie was the person who was making her life a misery. The sick bitch - if she was Vera's daughter, she should know the impact her actions would have on a woman in her fragile state. But then maybe that was her game?

Her only concern was to find Sam. She ran into the kitchen, looking for any sign that they'd been there recently. The toys were left scattered on the floor where they'd been playing.

Rosie looked in the corner; the pushchair had gone. Mackenzie had taken Sam out – but where? Then she saw it, a picture drawn in crayon of a person standing on a bridge with a road and cars underneath it. It was a simple drawing, of a stick lady. Nobody would think anything of it if they saw it. But Rosie knew what it meant, and she knew where Sam was now.

'Call the Uber back,' Rosie shouted at James as he joined her in the kitchen.

'Edward's alive,' he said. 'He's still breathing. But he's out cold – I'll call an ambulance. This is getting out of hand. The Uber guy is on his way to his next job.'

'Then we're going in my car,' Rosie said, her mind now intent on getting to Mackenzie. When she found that conniving witch, she'd throw her off the flyover herself.

CHAPTER TWENTY-SEVEN

'Should you be driving?' James asked.

'Fuck you, James!' Rosie cursed. 'She's got my son. She's trying to torment me. This has to end tonight.'

'Will you please keep the noise down out there?'

Rosie had taken her car keys from the hook in the kitchen and was now checking Edward for signs of life in the hallway. Her neighbour had heard the fun and games and was now standing in the doorway.

'What have you done?' she asked.

Rosie was so out of it, she wasn't entirely sure what she was imagining and what was real. She couldn't deal with her neighbour at that moment.

'Screw you!' she shouted. 'Get away from my house. This is nothing to do with you.'

'Steady, Rosie,' James urged.

'I'm calling the police. What have you done to that poor man? He needs help. I told the police you're insane. You're not fit to care for that child of yours.'

'Do what you want, but if you don't get out of my way, I'll run you down.'

'You're mad. I always knew you were.'

Rosie couldn't care less now; she just wanted to get to Sam. And if it meant driving again, so be it. James was saying something to appease her neighbour, but she didn't care any more. The ambulance was on its way, Edward was alive, and her only priority now was her child. If her neighbour had called the police, all to the good; they could lock up that cow Mackenzie and throw away the key.

Rosie removed the protective cover from her car, tossing it aside like a piece of rubbish. Then she clicked the remote unit on the small vehicle. It released the locks like it hadn't been sitting tucked on the drive for two years. Maybe if they'd taken her car to the leaving do two years ago – perhaps if she'd done the driving that night – none of this would ever have happened.

She put the key in the ignition and turned it. The engine groaned like it was unwilling to be disturbed from its slumber. She hadn't even thought about whether there'd be any juice left in the battery. She turned over the engine again, then again. James opened the passenger door and got in beside her. At first, she imagined it was Liam. It was as if they were going out to the shops before the baby – before the babies – were born.

Rosie wanted to scream and cry. She thought of Phoebe – poor Phoebe, who'd never even got her chance at life.

'You're playing with fire here, Rosie,' James said. 'Where are you going? I'm sure everything is okay. Mackenzie probably just went out for a walk with Sam.'

'Don't even say that to me!' Rosie screamed. The engine fired. 'I know what she's doing to me. I know what she's up to.'

'Rosie,' James urged gently, 'perhaps you're still struggling after your illness.'

'Don't you dare try to suggest this is all in my head!' Rosie shouted.

She forced the vehicle into reverse, crunching the gears as she did so. The car lurched backwards, screeching out into the road and smashing against a vehicle that was parked opposite her drive.

'Damn, Rosie, you didn't even look to see if it was clear. My door isn't shut properly either.'

James quickly pulled the door closed. Rosie ignored the collision and forced the gearstick into first, pulling the car round straight.

'Is this thing even taxed and insured?' James asked.

'It didn't make any bloody difference when we had our accident, so why should it make any difference now?' she replied. She knew she was out of control, fuelled by rage and frustration, but she didn't care. Anger at Liam, despair over Phoebe's death, fear of losing Sam; it all mixed to create a lethal cocktail of emotions which had been ignited by the sheer unfettered fury of realising Mackenzie was to blame for all those terrible things. She'd thought she was losing her mind.

The car roared along the road, Rosie not bothering to take it out of third gear.

'Where are we going?' James asked. 'You need to stop this, Rosie. You're going too far.'

'The bridge, we're going to the bridge. That's where the little cow has taken him. She's trying to taunt me. The spiteful bitch – I know what she's doing.'

Rosie swerved around the corner, clipping a second car as she focused on trying to remember the route. It seemed much more straightforward on foot. After another right turn, then two lefts, at last she arrived at the motorway flyover.

This was where she'd once considered killing herself, in a distant time. She'd even got as far as the other side of the barrier, with Sam in his pram behind her, ready to jump into the traffic below. All she could think of now was Sam's life – and that meant she had to live, if only for her son.

Rosie clipped the kerb as she pulled up at the side of the road. She didn't bother switching off the engine or applying the hand brake – the door was open, and she was out on the path in seconds.

'Where are you, you fucking bitch?'

Then she saw Mackenzie, holding Sam in her hands. She stared back at Rosie as the motorway traffic thundered below them, busy even at that time of night.

'Stop there!' Mackenzie shouted.

Rosie stopped dead. Mackenzie had placed Sam on the top of the metal fencing that ran along the flyover. She balanced him there, holding him firmly with her hands.

'Stay where you are,' Mackenzie cautioned. 'Sam and I are playing a game.'

'You're fucking mad!' Rosie screamed at her, fighting to be heard over the sound of the traffic below them. Their lights illuminated the bridge as they whizzed by at speed – lorries, cars, vans – each one a random bullet in a game of Russian roulette. If Sam were to fall, one of them could kill him in an instant. James was now standing behind her, at a distance.

'Hey, James!' Mackenzie shouted, as if she'd been expecting him.

Then Rosie watched as Mackenzie started to play a sick game with her son, his face turned to her, his back to the deadly motorway.

'Humpty Dumpty sat on a wall...'

'Don't you dare!' Rosie screamed, considering whether

to rush at Mackenzie. Sam was laughing, thinking it was all a game. He hadn't a clue how much peril he was in.

'Humpty Dumpty had a great fall...'

Mackenzie released one of her hands. Sam yelped with joy.

'No!' Rosie called, rushing forward.

'Steady, Rosie,' Mackenzie warned, moving her free hand to something that was tucked into the back of her trousers. All Rosie could focus on was the single hand that was holding her son, who was still balanced on the railing of the motorway bridge.

Mackenzie drew a small kitchen knife from behind her back. Rosie recognised it as one of her own. She was also vaguely aware now of police sirens in the distance; had her nosy neighbour finally done something useful?

Rosie's legs were weak, her mind a mess of confused thoughts and feelings. She could so easily cry, scream and collapse to the floor, craving the oblivion of her medication, yet she knew Sam needed her more than anybody in the world right now.

'Why are you doing this, Mackenzie? Why do you hate me so much? Vera is my friend. I love her. I owe her everything.'

'Because I can,' Mackenzie smiled.

With the knife in her hand, Mackenzie resembled the Chucky doll that had been sent as a gift for Sam's birthday. She had never seen anybody look so evil in her life.

'And because Mum cares for you loonies more than she ever bothered about me. But mostly because it's fun. You nutters don't know what we're doing to you most of the time.'

'Okay, Mackenzie,' James said. Rosie had almost

forgotten about him standing there, behind her. He was a useless piece of trash. He'd done nothing to help so far.

'All the king's horses and all the king's men, couldn't put Humpty together again...'

'Mackenzie, please, no!'

The sirens were almost upon them now.

'It's okay, Rosie, I'm only messing with you,' Mackenzie said. 'Here, take him from me.'

Rosie looked directly into Mackenzie's eyes and saw a look of evil and hatred that she'd not known before. One hand was clutching Sam's coat at its front. If she let him go, he'd tumble backwards into the traffic below. In her other hand was the knife. Was this a trick?

'It's okay Rosie. I won't hurt you. Come and get him. I was only messing with you. A girl's gotta have fun somehow. Here, take this knife from me.'

Rosie edged closer, cautious and fearful. Mackenzie held out the knife. The sirens were just around the corner now. They would be deafening when they got there.

As Rosie reached for the knife, Mackenzie thrust it at her gently. Sam moved backwards on the railing and Mackenzie steadied him. He laughed, believing the Humpty Dumpty game was continuing.

'It's alright, I'm joking,' Mackenzie said. 'Take it. Then I'll give you Sam.'

'They're here now!' James shouted. Rosie didn't know who he was talking to, as she focused on taking the knife. Mackenzie moved her hand to Sam, lifted him away from the railing and unceremoniously thrust him at Rosie. The knife dropped to the ground at her feet. She grasped Sam and hugged him close, crying with relief and exhilaration. Her child was finally safe.

Through her haze, Rose was aware of Mackenzie

running up to join James. Police cars screeched to a halt just behind them. As she hugged and kissed Sam, she caught sight of a distinctive pair of boots and heard the reassuring voice of DI Sarah Fletcher, trying to calm her down. Then there were screams. It was Mackenzie.

'She's going to jump with the baby – she told me. Look, she's got a knife. She's going to kill the baby!'

Rosie's head was swimming, her senses overloaded by the thundering traffic on the motorway below her, the sudden sound of the sirens and the tense activity from the surrounding police officers. DI Sarah Fletcher was moving slowly towards her, while Mackenzie kept on screaming that she was crazy, intent on killing her child.

The last thing she was aware of was Sarah Fletcher gently taking Sam from her arms, as a sudden panic that she might throw him into the traffic below gave way to an agonising pain in her chest that made her fall to her knees.

EPILOGUE

'There you are Rosie, darling. You're all sorted now.'

Vera finished wiping her eyes with a damp flannel and kissed her friend on the forehead.

'I never expected to see poor old Rosie here back at Trinity Heights. I thought she was going to sort herself out. She's lucky to have a friend like you, Mackenzie.'

Mackenzie smiled.

'I hope it helps when I visit the patients in their rooms, Mum. Some of them are so out of it on their meds. I don't know if I'm doing any good. If you think it helps, I'll keep doing it.'

'Rosie's going to need your friendship more than ever,' Vera replied, 'what with her dad in a home now and poor Sam with foster parents. It's such a terrible state of affairs.'

Vera moved the sheets back slightly from Rosie's chest and pulled back her gown a little.

'The marks are healing nicely now. Fancy tasering a woman in her distressed condition. No wonder she was in such a state.'

Vera covered up Rosie once again and straightened the few objects that had been placed on her bedside table. There was a framed photograph of Sam and one of her dad.

'Here's your new friend now. Fancy keeping him away from me all this time. He seems like such a nice chap – don't scare him off like all the others,' she said.

'Oh no, James is special,' Mackenzie replied.

'Hi Mrs Philpot,' James said, walking into the room. 'How's Rosie now, any better?'

'She'll have to stay sedated for some time,' Vera said. 'Who would have thought she'd threaten her baby? She told me she was finished with all those dark thoughts.'

'When will she get out of here?' James asked.

'Who knows?' Vera replied. 'She's been committed. Without her husband or her father to take care of her, she has nobody left to make decisions for her and advocate on her behalf. It's all in the hands of the social workers now. And I can't imagine that she'll get Sam back, not after what she tried to do; imagine threatening to cut your own child's throat with a kitchen knife?'

'I had to tell the police she said that, Mum. I felt terrible snitching her out. But I was doing it for Sam.'

James smiled at Mackenzie. He nodded at Rosie, whose hand had just flinched.

'You're good friends, both of you. Right, I've got other patients to see now, are you two fine with keeping Rosie here company? It'll do her good to hear your voices.'

Mackenzie and James nodded in unison and Vera left the room. A moment later, they began to laugh.

'Watch this,' Mackenzie said. 'Make sure the coast is clear.'

James checked the door.

'It's fine,' he said. 'Go ahead.'

Mackenzie moved the sheet down a little.

'Looks like the taser wound is healing nicely,' she laughed.

Rosie lay there, deadly still.

'Give it a try,' Mackenzie urged. 'She doesn't know you're doing it. You can get away with anything in this place when they're out of their heads on meds. Stroke her face. She won't even know you're doing it.'

James seemed nervous, like he needed some encouragement, but he did it anyway

'And she won't remember anything afterwards?' James asked.

'No, it's the best laugh ever!' Mackenzie replied. 'She didn't even realise who I was at work, stupid cow. Close the door, let's have some fun with her.'

'Hey, speaking of work, I'm keeping my job. David's bought back the company. Edward Logan is out on his arse, in spite of everybody thinking he was the victim of an attack by Rosie. That's so funny what you did there, leaving him in the hallway like that. It was a masterstroke. I've been searching for a woman like you all my life; we're soulmates, you and I.'

'And to think we'd never 'ave met if my mum hadn't had that fling with David. He used to come in here to visit Rosie the first time she was at Trinity Heights. She just used to lie like she is now, spaced out and shut off from the world. Mum took pity on him, I think – he used to sit here at visiting time, and Rosie would be boring as fuck like she is now. He should've felt her up a bit to pass the time. It was him who gave me the internship. What a sucker! I think he felt guilty when he packed my mum in. He said he was on the rebound after his wife died. Silly bugger.'

'Did you bring the meds?' James asked.

'Yeah, but we won't need to slip her any extras. Rosie is in here for a long time now. Once you get committed and there's nobody fighting for you, it's like throwing away the key. You didn't half dose her up that night; how much were you slipping into her drinks?'

'I told you, I used to work in a bar. I know how to mix up a good cocktail.'

James and Mackenzie laughed. Rosie's finger twitched as their cackles filled the room.

'So, what are we going to do next?' James asked.

'What do you mean?' Mackenzie replied.

'Well, that was fun, screwing with Rosie. I want to do it again.'

'It's not enough messing about with her and saying horrible things to her?'

'No, I want to fuck up somebody else's life.'

Mackenzie kissed James on the cheek and grinned at him. 'There's a young guy down the hallway. He's about to get released from the unit any day now. I gave him a snog in his room last night, and now he thinks he's in love with me. How about we work on him?'

'I like it!' James said. 'This is much more fun than a night in watching Netflix. Shall we go and see him now?'

'Yes, let's. Let him know you're my boyfriend – that'll screw with his head.'

'I'll kiss you in the room while he's there. Let's have a bet. I reckon he'll be back in here within a week.'

'Touch my butt when we're in there, and I think we can squeeze it into five days.'

'Done! It's a bet,' James grinned, standing up to leave the room.

'I told my mum you were a keeper,' Mackenzie said as she took his hand and they moved towards the door.

As they left the room, Rosie's hand twitched.

If you enjoyed this book, you'll love the Morecambe Bay series of psychological thrillers. Nine books and non-stop suspense. Available in paperback and e-book formats.

AUTHOR NOTES

Two Years After is the first psychological thriller I've written that didn't have a positive outcome for the protagonist. I seldom end stories with a completely happy ending, but I wanted this book to be different. It's supposed to leave you – the reader – with an unsettled, queasy feeling. You've just witnessed the grinning face of pure evil, after all. Poor old Rosie, what a terrifying experience for such a fabulous character.

So what would make me put you through all of that as a reader? Well, it was inspired by the lingering feeling I had at the end of the film Funny Games, an Austrian psychological thriller directed by Michael Haneke in 1997 (it has a great Wikipedia page).

I think that film – on first-time viewing – is one of the most tense and unsettling movies I've ever watched. There is a USA version too, with the same director, but I recommend the original if you don't mind the subtitles.

I wanted to leave you, my ever-suffering reader, with that same realisation that you get at the end of Funny

Games: a sense that this is going to happen again to another innocent victim.

As well as being a dark thriller, Two Years After condenses many of my thoughts and experiences on corporate life. I've been a teacher, a sales representative, a waiter, a shop assistant, a DJ, a radio presenter, producer and journalist and a digital development manager in my working life. I was keen to set this book in the workplace and convey many of the horrors that we subject ourselves to in order to earn a living. I should stress that it's a work of fiction, none of these things happened in real life.

I'll bet you'll recognise a lot of what goes on: the characters, the pettiness, the scenarios. That's why I chose *Going to work can be hell* as the tagline for the book. Many of us have that same thought every Monday morning.

A serious issue that I wanted to deal with in the book is that of mental health. This is a hot topic at the moment, and I'm delighted to see how openly people discuss it these days. When I started work, you'd never admit to anxiety, depression or stress for fear of being sidelined. I'm happy to see these matters being dealt with openly. I believe we need to treat good mental health in the same way that we approach our physical health.

Rosie struggles with the pressures placed upon her; to provide for her son, to convince the social workers of her suitability as a mother, to pick up her career and to keep dragging herself out of bed, day after day.

I read an excellent article on this topic by one of my favourite pop stars, Adam Ant, several years ago, when he released his book, *Stand and Deliver*. Do an online search for the article *Adam Ant: back from the brink* in The Telegraph. You'll see that's what Rosie's experiences are based upon.

It's funny how these things influence you as a writer. In Rosie's case, her despair, anxiety and depression are caused by the death of a child, the demise of her husband and her physical injuries and trauma. She's put in a vice-like situation where social workers are watching her on the one hand, and her employer is cutting off her money, despite David's best efforts.

Although I place all sorts of obstacles in her way, I like Rosie. She's a great mother placed in an impossible situation.

Mackenzie is based upon characters like Beverley Allitt, who was involved in a very high profile case in the United Kingdom. She is a child serial killer, and I think it's fair to say that the terms Munchausen syndrome and Munchausen syndrome by proxy became better known by the general population in my country as a result of the reporting of that case.

I also wanted to reflect the fact that things like that can happen; misuse of prescription drugs, lack of supervision, and ongoing problems persisting without a challenge. My book is purely fiction, but this stuff happens in real life. Mackenzie's relationship with James is a spark of evil collusion, as it was with Ian Brady and Myra Hindley, and Fred and Rosemary West.

However much I left you feeling unsettled at the end of Two Years After, I do hope that you enjoyed reading the story as much as I enjoyed dreaming up the scenarios. I had a lot of fun writing the scene where they're all squashed into the small car. Once again, this is inspired by a real-life experience, only the person who was almost sick was me.

It was in my days as a cub reporter, in the back of a Granada TV car, travelling at some speed along a single track road in my home county of Cumbria. It's called Hard-

knott Pass – look it up online. We were stopping and starting, pulling into passing places to let other vehicles get by,
and in a rush to record a TV report at the Sellafield nuclear
site.

I thought I was going to be sick all over the TV
reporter's posh suit – imagine that on the six o'clock news!
Luckily I managed to hold on to my stomach, but in my
story, Neil Jennings doesn't.

If you liked this story and want to stay in touch, I'd be
delighted if you registered for my email updates at
https://paulteague.net/thrillers, as that's where I share
news of what I'm writing and tell you about any reader
discounts and freebies that are available.

Paul Teague

ALSO BY PAUL J. TEAGUE

Morecambe Bay Trilogy 1

Book 1 - Left For Dead

Book 2 - Circle of Lies

Book 3 - Truth Be Told

Morecambe Bay Trilogy 2

Book 4 - Trust Me Once

Book 5 - Fall From Grace

Book 6 - Bound By Blood

Morecambe Bay Trilogy 3

Book 7 - First To Die

Book 8 - Nothing To Lose

Book 9 - Last To Tell

Note: The Morecambe Bay trilogies are best read in the order shown above.

Don't Tell Meg Trilogy

Features DCI Kate Summers and Steven Terry.

Book 1 - Don't Tell Meg

Book 2 - The Murder Place

Book 3 - The Forgotten Children

Standalone Thrillers

Dead of Night

One Last Chance

No More Secrets

So Many Lies

Friends Who Lie

Now You See Her

NO MORE SECRETS PREVIEW

Spean Bridge, July 1999

Katy watched as the cottage burned. Elijah was in there, unable to escape from the wooden structure as it was engulfed in flames. The fire was ferocious in the wind, with huge flares sweeping across the garden, keeping the huddle of horrified onlookers at bay. The air was filled with the crackle of burning timber and the sobbing of the five friends, distraught at the thought of Elijah trapped inside.

Driven back by the searing heat, they watched in terror, unable to think of any action they could take to extinguish the inferno. They were forced to sit it out and wait until the horror ended. Elijah didn't stand a chance. There was nothing to stop the flames once they'd started, and they consumed the building in less than half an hour.

There were no phone boxes nearby. The cabin nestled at the foot of a hill, surrounded by trees, and at the end of a long, winding track. Even if help could have been summoned, it would have been too late. They were too far away from the nearest town.

It had seemed like such a good idea: two weeks in the Scottish Highlands, a log cabin in the middle of nowhere, and a car boot filled with booze. They'd finished their year one exams, they had a long summer ahead of them, and they were in love – young, idealistic love, their whole lives yet to live. They had nearly four months away from university and nothing to do with all that time.

Five of them had piled into the car – it was a wonder there was any room for the clothes and toiletries. They didn't care, all they could think of was two weeks of sleeping in, laughter and drinking. But it all took a turn for the worse. The easy-come, easy-go bubble of university life quickly evaporated as the reality of living in a cabin with an erratic boiler and night-time visits from the local vermin set in. The laughter turned to bitching, the booze remained unopened in the fridge, and relationships became tense. What had seemed like too short a time to go on holiday soon turned into an eternity. Two weeks became a lifetime and plans to share a student house in the new term began to look hasty and ill-conceived.

But it never should have come to this. They watched and wept as the wooden structure was transformed into a smoking, charred ruin. Elijah was in there somewhere. There would be nothing left of him, the flames were so fierce. The squabbles seemed so petty now. How had they let it get so out of hand?

Eventually, in the darkness of the night time, the emergency services arrived, alerted by a farmer across the valley. He'd thought it was a woodland fire, started by careless campers. It turned out to be much worse.

When the police got there, they found five shocked friends, standing and watching the scene before them, stunned at what had just happened. It would take them a long time to recover from what they'd seen.

In spite of the tears, Elijah's death was no freak accident, even though it would be sadly recorded as such by the Sheriff. There was a reason why Elijah hadn't escaped to safety, even though he should have got away well before the flames took a grip. Nobody could understand why he hadn't got out, but there was nothing to suggest anything but a tragic sequence of events.

The repercussions of that day would be felt for many years to come. There was always a lingering doubt among the friends, a feeling that somebody could have helped him on that terrible day. Elijah's death could have been avoided. But not everyone had told the truth that night.

No More Secrets is available as a paperback or e-book.

ABOUT THE AUTHOR

Hi, I'm Paul Teague, the author of the Morecambe Bay series and the Don't Tell Meg trilogy, as well as several other standalone psychological thrillers such as One Last Chance, Dead of Night and No More Secrets.

I'm a former broadcaster and journalist with the BBC, but I have also worked as a primary school teacher, a disc jockey, a shopkeeper, a waiter and a sales rep.

I've read thrillers all my life, starting with Enid Blyton's Famous Five series as a child, then graduating to James Hadley Chase, Harlan Coben, Linwood Barclay and Mark Edwards.

Let's get connected!
https://paulteague.net

Printed in Great Britain
by Amazon

80590897R00120